Emma Benedict wants to be a really good nurse, a modern-day Florence Nightingale, but somehow all she does results in chaos. And when she comes into contact with Senior Registrar Garrard Blair life becomes almost unbearable . . .

NOT AGAIN, NURSE!

BY

LEONIE CRAIG

MILLS & BOON LIMITED
London · Sydney · Toronto

First published in Great Britain 1984
by Mills & Boon Limited, 15–16 Brook's Mews,
London W1A 1DR

ISBN 0 263 74572 4

Set in 11 on 11½ pt Linotron Times
03/0284–52,164

Photoset by Rowland Phototypesetting Ltd
Bury St Edmunds, Suffolk
Made and printed in Great Britain by
Richard Clay (The Chaucer Press) Ltd
Bungay, Suffolk

For another Emma, and for Amy.

CHAPTER ONE

'*Si . . . lent night, ho . . . ly night.*'

'Nurse Benedict.'

Emma Benedict's hand, poised in the act of filling a jug with water, shook as Sister Meredith's voice reached her and that stout figure stood framed in the doorway.

She wasn't quite sure how it happened, but by some apparently magical process her hand and the jug parted company, sending it crashing to the floor and her gaze rose, shudderingly, from her uniform to the puddle spreading ever wider across the floor at her feet.

Sister Meredith's eyes were closed briefly in a swift prayer for patience, wondering what she had ever done, what authority she had ever flouted, that she should have been punished with a nurse like Emma Benedict. Yet she had to quell a strong urge to laugh as the girl stood before her, a dripping picture of abject misery.

Emma's hand rose automatically to the cap which always sat so beautifully on everyone else's hair but which seemed to defy the laws of gravity when it came to her mop of unruly auburn curls.

Water dripped down the front of her blue gingham uniform into her shoes and she grimaced. She had done it again. Her large brown eyes filled with tears and she blinked them back furiously. And she had actually thought she was going to get through one day without having incurred Sister's wrath.

'Yes, Sister. Sorry Sister.' Her mouth quivered beneath Sister Meredith's steely gaze.

'I don't doubt the entire ward appreciates your efforts to enrich our lives musically, Nurse, but isn't September just a little premature for Christmas carols?'

Dark lashes covered the brown eyes. 'Sorry, Sister, I was just practising for the hospital choir.'

'Well far be it for me to discourage your efforts, but you are here to work and whilst you are still on duty your mind should be concentrated solely on the job in hand. Do I make myself perfectly clear?'

'Oh yes, Sister.'

'Then may I ask what you were doing in the kitchen anyway?'

'Mr Douglas asked for a drink, Sister, and I was just making a jug of orange juice.'

'I see, and in the meantime what about Mr Langley?' She saw the look of confusion momentarily cloud the girl's face. 'You do remember Mr Langley? He's the man with the red face. You'll find him sitting on the edge of his bed waiting for the bedpan which you apparently promised him fifteen minutes ago. I assure you, he is not feeling very happy.'

Emma groaned. 'Oh no.' It had completely slipped her mind. She had been hurrying down the ward to fetch it when Mr Douglas had called her over to ask for a drink and had started showing her the photographs of his daughter's new baby. It was no excuse, of course, as Sister's look of displeasure made amply clear. 'I'll get it straight away, Sister.'

'That won't be necessary. Male Nurse Richards has attended to it. I would suggest, Nurse, that you clear up this mess, then go and change your uniform and report back to me on the ward in ten minutes.'

'Yes, Sister.' A sigh of resignation accompanied the words as the door closed behind the ample, navy-clad figure. 'And I suppose that means another ticking off.' She squelched across to the cupboard, took out a mop and dealt furiously with the puddle. She was just in the process of making more orange juice when Mike Richards walked into the kitchen.

He was tall, thin and boyishly attractive but Emma wasn't looking at his blond good looks as she stood, crossly trying to wring water out of her apron.

'Come on, buck up, Benedict. Sister's really on the war-path. Here, let me take that. You go and change.'

She relinquished her hold on the jug, sniffed loudly and brushed a tear from her eye. 'Blast.'

Mike Richards grinned. 'Oh, come on, it's not that bad. You know Meredith's bark is always worse than her bite.'

'Hm, not where I'm concerned it isn't. That's the second time this week. I'm supposed to see her in ten minutes and if she reports me to the DNS I'm finished. Oh Mike, what is it about me? I don't seem to be able to do anything without causing chaos and it's not as if I mean to.'

'I'm sure it's not really that bad.' He studied her seriously. Emma Benedict was a pretty little thing. Barely five feet two inches in her black-stockinged feet, twenty years old and looking, at this moment, scarcely more than sixteen. He felt the protective instinct surge in him and proffered his hanky when the search for her own obviously proved fruitless. 'Perhaps you're trying too hard.'

She sniffed and blew hard. 'It's just that I want so desperately to be a nurse. I always have. I mean a really good nurse.'

'Don't we all?'

'Yes, but you don't understand, I always grew up with this idea of myself as a sort of modern-day Florence Nightingale, tending the sick.'

'Soothing fevered brows?' he mocked, gently.

Her chin rose fiercely. 'I'm not playing at it. It's what I want to do. I'd die if I had to give it up because I wasn't good enough.'

Mike shifted his weight from where he was perched on the table and put a comforting arm round her shoulders. 'I do know what you mean, you know. Just because I'm a man doesn't mean I don't have the same dedication to the job.'

She turned her face miserably up to his. 'But why does it keep going wrong?' She gulped furiously to get rid of the lump in her throat. 'I only have to hear Sister's voice and I make a complete hash of what I'm doing and I'm not really that stupid. I know I can do the job. It's just that I go to pieces and always at the wrong time.'

'It won't go on for ever. This is only your first year. We all go through it. As you get more experience you'll become more confident, believe me.'

She sighed. 'I wish I could, but I don't think I'm even going to make it to my second year at this rate.'

'Rubbish.' He kissed her cheek and she blushed furiously. She liked Mike and if he asked her out she had already made up her mind she would say yes. But the chance didn't come.

The door flew open and a tall, white-coated figure with a distinctly cross expression on his handsome face demanded crossly, 'Where the devil is all the staff on this ward? I want to see Sister urgently and I can't find her anywhere.' His incredibly blue eyes narrowed as Emma ejected herself forcibly from Mike's embrace and she felt her cheeks burn at the silent mockery in his gaze. She resented it. Housemen were always coming and going, full of their own importance. And this one, she decided roundly, was obviously worse than most. The fact that he also happened to be vaguely good looking, well, actually quite good looking, probably gave him the idea that he only had to open his mouth and anything in skirts would fall at his feet. Her mouth compressed with a determination not to fall into that category, which made it all the more galling as she found herself taking in the gaunt face and craggily handsome looks and felt a tingle of excitement run through her. She felt her eyes drawn to the shock of brown hair and the eyes which flashed like steel, and drew herself up to her full height in an attempt to lessen the jelly-like quivering of her knees. He stood with one hand in his pocket but she wasn't fooled by the casual stance. He had witnessed the scene between herself and Mike and had drawn his own, obviously misguided, conclusions.

A nerve pulsed in the square jaw as he looked scathingly at Mike.

'If you can spare the time from your other . . .

activities, perhaps you'd be good enough to find
Sister and inform her that I'd like to have a word
with her urgently. If it won't be too much trouble.'

Emma felt her temper rise. There was really no
need for him to be quite so sarcastic. She felt sorry
for Mike who murmured quietly, 'Not at all, sir, I'll
find Sister for you now.' And with a swift look in
her direction he was gone.

The small kitchen seemed suddenly smaller as
Emma found herself coming under even closer
scrutiny. 'I don't remember seeing you here before.
Are you new?'

It was hardly surprising he didn't know her, she
thought caustically, since doctors were gods and
junior nurses were taught to remain silent and to
merge completely into the background while
rounds took place.

Her chin rose. 'No, sir . . . Well, yes . . . that
is I've been on Men's Surgical for about three
weeks.'

'Really?' Dark brows rose. 'I'm surprised the
ward has survived intact for that long.' She felt the
hot colour surge into her cheeks but he gave her no
chance to utter the protest which hung on her lips.
'I suggest, Nurse, that you get out of that uniform
unless you were planning on returning to the ward
in that state.'

She stared with horror down at the sodden state
of her uniform. Its appearance certainly hadn't
been improved by Mike's comforting embrace.

'Oh lord. I forgot.'

'I don't doubt it.' His lip curled contemptuously.
'Perhaps if you were to keep your mind on your
work instead of on the opposite sex and the intri-

cacies of arranging your next date, this ward might be run more efficiently.'

For a moment Emma was left speechless but it was enough. He was already striding away, leaving her shaking with fury and wishing she had never set eyes on him. Well, with a bit of luck she never would again although how she was to achieve that miracle was something to ponder on at a later date. There was just time to sprint over to the Nurses' Home to change her uniform before the executioner's axe fell and lopped off her future prospects.

Breathing hard she reached the ward two minutes after the time allotted by Sister Meredith, but with a sigh of relief she managed to slip in unnoticed as she saw Sister briefly occupied in escorting an all-too-familiar figure as he made his examination of one of the patients. Oh no, it couldn't be. He's going to haunt me for the rest of my life, she thought.

She skirted deftly past the curtains which were drawn round the bed, mercifully hiding her from view, and when he left five minutes later she purposely busied herself by tidying out one of the lockers, kneeling on one black-stockinged knee so that as he swept by she caught only a glimpse of his trousered leg. The urge to sink her teeth into it flashed briefly through her mind and she giggled. The footsteps paused briefly and unwillingly her gaze rose to be met by a cool stare before he passed on. And he didn't even recognise me, she thought with an unreasoned pang of resentment as she bundled the contents of the locker hastily back into place and forced the door to a close.

A voice hissed down at her. 'Nurse, I say, Nurse.'

She looked up peevishly as a hand jabbed at her shoulder. 'Yes, Mr Thomas, what is it now?'

The florid face was looking slightly put out. 'Nothing, Nurse, only you've just put a bunch of grapes in my sponge bag and a bar of soap in the fruit dish.'

With a groan she retrieved the offending items and saw Sister bearing down upon her. 'Oh blast, I was hoping she had forgotten,' she muttered. Automatically she checked her cap and straightened the elasticated belt at her waist before scuttling along the ward and following the beckoning hand in the office.

Sister Meredith sat at the desk, her hands clasped ominously. 'I am not pleased, Nurse.'

'No, Sister.'

'And the reason I am not pleased is because I have come to the conclusion, Nurse, that you are a disruptive influence upon this ward.'

Emma stared at her feet. There was a large scuff mark on one of her shoes where she had knelt down. 'Yes, Sister,' she mumbled.

'I do not like disruptive influences on my ward, Nurse.'

Emma bit her lip, forcing herself to meet the stern gaze, sighing heavily. 'I do try . . .'

'Apparently with great success.' Sister Meredith's tone was tinged heavily with sarcasm.

'Oh no, Sister, I didn't mean . . .'

'I know exactly what you mean, Nurse Benedict, but the fact remains that wherever you are there is disorder. Whatever you do results in chaos. I cannot have my ward run in such a manner, Nurse, and I see only one possible solution. One of us must change and I assure you I have every intention that it shall be you.' Clasped hands were withdrawn as Sister Meredith rose and crossed to the window from which she could see every square inch of the ward. In the uneasy silence Emma quickly brushed the scuffed shoe against her stocking and stood miserably wondering whether her presence had been entirely forgotten. She found herself studying the short, ample figure and the iron-grey hair upon which the neat, white cap sat as if anchored by magnets into its precise place. Or possibly it knew better than to fall off, she thought.

'How long have you been with us, Nurse?'

Emma felt a wave of cold despair run through her. Was this it then? 'Almost a year, Sister.'

'I'm aware that you've been at St Clement's for almost a year, Nurse, I meant how long on this particular ward?'

'Sorry, Sister. About three weeks.'

The grey brows rose dejectedly. 'Only that long? It seems more. And do you enjoy your work?'

'Oh yes, Sister, I love it.'

'I don't doubt that you do, Nurse, but I think it's time we both faced the possibility that you may not be suited to nursing.'

Emma turned white. 'Oh no, Sister. You don't mean . . .'

'At the moment I am not implying anything. I am simply saying that things cannot go on as they are. I have a ward full of sick people, which must be run smoothly and efficiently if each of their individual needs is to be met and the standards of this hospital maintained. I am seriously concerned that those standards are not being met, Nurse, and that much of the blame must lie with you.' Sister looked at her sharply. 'I appreciate your enthusiasm, Nurse Benedict, but enthusiasm alone is not enough. Nursing requires a dedication and a tireless effort and it seems to me that the efforts of the rest of my staff are being hindered by your . . . by your apparent inability to perform even the simplest task without disrupting the entire ward in the process.'

Emma felt as if the lump in her throat would choke her. 'Yes, Sister. I'm sorry, Sister. I really don't know why it happens.'

'Today you forgot Mr Langley's bedpan, thereby causing him not only a lot of discomfort but also a considerable loss of dignity, and all because your mind was not properly on your work. Yesterday you left the bathroom tap running and almost flooded the entire ward, and last week you actually managed to lose a patient who was supposed to be going down to X-ray.'

'But I only left him for a moment, Sister, and he went to the toilet without telling . . .'

'I'm really not interested in excuses, Nurse. I'm afraid they aren't good enough.'

'No, Sister.' Unshed tears threatened to gush like the bathroom tap. 'Does this mean . . . that I'm to be asked to leave?'

Laura Meredith frowned as she stared at the girl's lowered head. In spite of everything she liked Emma Benedict. Upon occasions, unobserved, she had watched her and had noticed how popular she was even with the most irascible patient. But popularity wasn't enough, and for how long could she go on in the mere hope that some day this girl would prove her right in the belief that somewhere, beneath all the clumsiness, a truly first-class nurse was only waiting to emerge? Laura Meredith was seldom wrong. In thirty years she had learned how to judge the wheat from the chaff, but in Emma Benedict's case she still couldn't be sure.

She frowned, glancing at the clock and longing for the time when she could go off-duty, to her homely little flat, and take off the stiff white collar and neat, navy dress. Her voice gave no hint of her feelings.

'I have decided not to speak to the DNS this time.' She felt herself almost flinch at the look of gratitude which spread across the white face.

'Oh, thank you, Sister.'

Her hand rose. 'I said "this time", Nurse. You must appreciate that things cannot go on as they have. I'm simply giving you another chance, that's all. It's up to you to take it, otherwise I have to warn you I think your nursing career may well be over and that would be a pity. I suspect that one day you might do very well.'

Emma flushed with shocked disbelief. 'Oh, thank you, Sister.'

'Don't thank me, Nurse, except by proving to me that you can do the job, that's all I ask.' She picked up a file from the desk. 'Now, will you please take this over to Miss Baxter's office. It's the latest off-duty list, and tell her I'll let her have the holiday rota tomorrow morning at the latest.'

'Yes, Sister.' Feeling as if her feet had wings, Emma sped along the corridor and down the stairs towards the office of the Director of Nursing Services. Miss Baxter eyed the lists gratefully.

'Thank Sister for me will you, and tell her I hope

to be at the meeting tomorrow night after all,' she said.

'Yes, Miss Baxter.'

She returned up the stairs, her shoes making odd little squeaking sounds as she walked. She glanced in at Men's Medical as she passed and recognised Staff Nurse Carson's mauve-clad figure. The corridor was quiet and she hummed softly to herself, unaware of the tall, white-coated figure walking some yards ahead, obviously deeply involved in the mound of case notes he was carrying.

The swing doors answered the slight pressure of her hand as she went through, making her grand entrance. One day, when she was the DNS, staff would leap to attention at the mere sight of her. The loud bellow of pain as the doors swung open froze her to the spot in horror as she recognised the voice.

'Nurse!'

Oh no, it couldn't be. Fate couldn't be that cruel, not twice in one day. She watched in a horrified trance as pages slithered under the door and came to rest at her feet. Bending to pick them up she was conscious of the feet which suddenly planted themselves in front of her and she rose to see the gleam of fury and pain in the eyes which stared down at her with loathing and slowly dawning recognition.

'You?' he looked as if he would like to throttle her. 'I might have known it. You crazy little fool.'

She tried to speak but the fury in his eyes silenced her.

'Didn't anyone ever teach you to check before you launch yourself through a swing door, just in case someone might happen to be on the other side?'

'I'm sorry,' she said in a strangled voice. 'Really I am.'

'Sorry?' Contempt crashed about her ears. 'My God, I've come to the conclusion you're a walking disaster area. You're not safe to be let out on your own, particularly in a hospital.' He gritted his teeth and rubbed at his elbow.

Instinctively she reached up to tug at his sleeve. 'Oh, you're hurt. Let me see.'

He drew in a sharp, choking breath and seemed to be making a supreme effort to control himself. 'Leave it alone before you do any more damage. I am a doctor and perfectly capable of diagnosing for myself whether there are any broken bones or not. I suggest you get out of my sight, Nurse Benedict, before I bow to the temptation of putting you over my knee and giving you the spanking which you thoroughly deserve.'

Shock widened her brown eyes. He didn't mean it. He wouldn't dare. But something in the way he looked at her warned her not to put it to the test. Without a backward glance she turned and fled, and it was only when she reached Men's Surgical that she realised she was still clutching the papers she had picked up.

CHAPTER TWO

'OF ALL the pompous, bad-tempered idiots! How was I to know he was on the other side of the doors?' Emma groaned as she eased off her shoe and viewed a naked toe sticking through the hole in her tights with unwarranted frustration. 'Oh hell, now I'll have to go and change and I'll never make it in time. I'm due back on the ward in fifteen minutes.' She tugged at the nylon and screeched as a ladder shot up to her knee. 'And it's all his fault.'

Sally Faulkener consulted her watch, drained her coffee and frowned. 'Ten minutes actually. And how on earth do you make out it's all his fault?'

'Well of course it is,' Emma snapped. 'Life was complicated enough before he came along and pushed his way into it. Now it's unbearable and I just know he'll have it in for me.'

'Oh, rubbish. Anyway, I shouldn't think he even knows who you are.'

'Oh yes he does. He's the sort of man who knows everything, and in particular those things he's not supposed to know. Honestly, I've been expecting a summons to Miss Baxter's office since yesterday afternoon to hear I'm being drummed out of the service.' Tears of frustration belied the laughter. 'It isn't fair, it really isn't.'

'Well, I think you're making far too much of it.' Sally tucked a pin back into her blonde hair. 'Whoever this monster is, doctors—and especially junior

20

doctors—just don't bother indulging in personal vendettas against nurses.' She got to her feet, quiet laughter in her attractive blue eyes. 'Believe me, as far as they're concerned we don't even exist.'

'Well this one certainly knows I exist. He's probably got a black eye and broken fingers to prove it, and the way he looked at me I should think my features are imprinted on his memory for ever. I didn't stay to find out, though.' Her eyes widened. 'He actually threatened me with physical violence.'

'I wonder why,' Sally's mouth quivered. 'And are you sure you don't know who this monster is?'

'I haven't a clue. Not that that means anything. Put someone in a white coat and they all look the same to me. I've seen him on the ward but then people are always coming in and out. It's like the army—if it wears a white coat, bow and scrape.'

'Poor Benedict.' Sally eyed her friend ruefully. 'Look, come on, I've got to be back on Women's Med too, but I can let you have a new pair of tights if you want to pop up to the changing-room with me. You'll just about make it if we hurry. Otherwise I suggest you tuck your foot back in your shoes and hope the hole doesn't get any worse. With a bit of luck Sister may not notice.'

'She'll notice. Sister Meredith has the eyes of a hawk. I can feel them boring into me the minute I come within a hundred yards of her.'

Shuffling her foot into her shoe she followed the tall, slim girl whose blonde hair was coiled attractively into a bun and whose apron still looked spotless over the pink dress of a second-year nurse. They reached the changing-room where she changed into the new tights and just managed to walk, smugly, on to the ward as Sister Meredith was eyeing the clock.

'Oh Nurse Benedict, there you are.' Emma caught the conspiratorial look of sympathy flung in her direction by Sue Harper as she hurried past, before Sister's hand beckoned, and she mentally ticked off the sins of omission or otherwise which she might have perpetrated during her lunch break. 'Come along quickly.' A brisk note in Sister's voice advised no dawdling. 'I want all those lockers swabbed down and tidied up before Mr Blair makes his round. They're an absolute disgrace and he's such a stickler for efficiency he'll be bound to notice.'

Emma's eyes boggled. 'But he does his round in fifteen minutes, Sister.'

'Then you'll have to get a move on, won't you, Nurse. Oh and for heaven's sake, try and persuade Mr Mortimer that we are not a public lending library and to put some of his books away.'

'Yes, Sister.' She fled to the task, mentally trying to remember which of the consultants Mr Blair was.

'And, Nurse.' A finger rose, warningly. 'Try to bear in mind our little talk yesterday.'

She gulped, 'Yes, Sister,' and fled, rolling up her sleeves and donning cuffs before setting about wiping the lockers and removing those objects which were, for some totally incomprehensible reason, offensive to the eyes of Senior Registrars.

'You take this end of the ward, I'll take the other.' Sue bustled out of the kitchen with a basin of hot, soapy water. 'That way we'll be done in half the time.'

Shooting a look of gratitude over her shoulder,

Emma bent to the task, not without some assistance from the occupant of the bed.

'Sister got her bossy boots on today, 'as she?' Sam Hackett laughed wheezily.

Emma flung a look in Sister's direction and calculated the distance to be safe. 'I suppose you could say that. Oh Mr Hackett, what on earth is this?'

'This' was held aloft and Emma wrinkled her nose as the old man stared in bewilderment.

'Oh lor, so that's where them grapes got to. I keeps telling the missus not to bring 'em. Can't abide the things. Wretched seeds gets under me plate. But she will 'ave it. People in 'ospital gotta 'ave grapes. I say to her, I says, bring us a bloody pint, woman, and I'll be out of 'ere and *you* can eat the bloody grapes. But no . . .'

'Well you're not really allowed beer, Mr Hackett.'

'Now don't you start, Nurse. It's bad enough, 'aving them there doctors tellin' me what I can't 'ave. I'd like to tell a few of them toffee-nosed b . . .'

'Mr Hackett!'

'. . . gentlemen what they can do for a change.'

Emma bent her head to hide her laughter. 'Yes, well wouldn't we all, Mr Hackett, only don't let Sister hear you say so or life won't be worth living. Anyway, you'll be going home soon, won't you?'

'Ar. Come the end of the week, all being well.'

'Lucky you.' She sighed despondently.

'Aw come on, cheer up! It ain't as bad as all that.'

'No, of course it isn't. It's just that some days are worse than others.' She polished vigorously. 'I'll remove these grapes then, before Sister sees them, only next time, if you'd just let one of the nurses know, she can dispose of them for you.'

'Yes, well that's what I meant to do, but I forgot, and then I 'ad to push 'em out of sight when the wife arrived again. Don't want to 'urt her feelings.'

'Never mind,' Emma smiled. 'I'd better get on. I'm not exactly in Sister's good books.'

She fled to the kitchen with the offending heap of grapes oozing through a soggy paper bag and by some miracle the remaining lockers were finished minutes before the arrival of the Senior Registrar.

A look of satisfaction settled over Emma's face and was removed as the swing doors began to open and Sister's voice, cracking like ice, admonished, 'Nurse, your cuffs.'

With a quick gasp of horror she raced back to the kitchen, removed her cuffs and rolled down her sleeves and presented herself back on the ward just in time to see a white-coated, masculine figure disappearing behind the curtains which were drawn hastily round one of the beds.

She stood, hands clasped behind her, wondering how she could best merge into the background, and nearly giggled aloud at the thought that she could always hop into one of the beds, or under one.

Beside her Sue Harper cast her a warning look. 'For heaven's sake, what's the matter?'

'I was just wondering how Mr Hackett would react if I were to hurl myself under the covers beside him.'

'I should think he'd have a heart attack,' came the hissed response just as the curtains swished open and a figure stepped out.

Without the flicker of an eyelid the steely gaze

fixed itself firmly on Emma's face. She felt sick but there was certainly no escape, not with Sister standing there, glaring at her furiously.

'More than likely, Nurse. I hope for your sake and the patients' that you think seriously before undertaking any such course of action.'

Emma gazed with cold fascination at the two bandaged fingers and her eyes closed as she wished him, or herself, a million miles away. It didn't work. When she opened them again he was still there. Lean and ridiculously good looking and eyeing her with the kind of cold ruthlessness which made her wish she could crawl under a stone.

'It was a joke.' Her voice sounded shrill and it died as Sister flung a look of fury in her direction and wrenched the curtains back with a violence which nearly tore them from their fittings.

'I will see you later, Nurse, in my office.'

'Yes, Sister.' Cowed, she hardly dared look at the saturnine face of Garrard Blair. She hated him. She wished she'd broken all his fingers when she'd had the chance. The dark eyes glittered dangerously and she had the horrid suspicion that he had actually read her thoughts. Oh well, if she was going to be hung it might as well be for a sheep as for a lamb—not that there was anything even remotely sheep-like about the Senior Registrar. He was definitely more the predator type.

'Shall we get on with the round, Sister.' He smiled, Emma thought, with the kind of smile that would have turned her heart over if she hadn't disliked him so much, and she felt vaguely sickened to see that Sister fell for it.

'Certainly, Mr Blair. This is Mr Harris, he hopes

to be going home tomorrow.' Her gaze warned
Emma not to move, not even to blink until they
were safely out of sight.

The moment the curtains swished round the next
bed she gulped hard, told herself firmly that she
wasn't going to cry and promptly burst into tears.
There was only one place of refuge. Ignoring Mr
Hackett's cheery offer of his shoulder, she made a
dive for the linen room and wept over a pile of
sheets. Perhaps Sister was right, perhaps she *wasn't*
cut out to be a nurse. Not that it mattered now
anyway, since Mr Garrard Blair had finally decided
the matter for her.

CHAPTER THREE

'I HATE him! I hate him!' She plumped sheets furiously into an untidy pile as the linen cupboard doors shuddered open behind her. Her startled, tear-filled eyes rose in horror to see the angry features of Garrard Blair glaring at her from the doorway.

'I had a feeling I might find you in here.'

She shivered beneath the glacial stare, backing away a step.

'How dare you leave the ward in the middle of my round, without Sister's permission and certainly without mine?'

It was a question Emma asked herself as colour rushed into her face and she eased a tear away with one finger. She knew from the grimness of his expression that he was very angry and the effect of those dark, steely eyes reduced her knees to quivering jelly. She struggled to find words, knowing miserably that nothing she said could possibly excuse the enormity of what she had done.

'I . . . I'm sorry.' She sniffed hard, fumbled for a hanky and blew her nose hard.

'Sorry?' She flinched and his glance tightened ominously. 'Why do nurses always skulk in the linen cupboard when they want to have a good cry?'

Her chin rose defensively. She wanted to say 'Because it's the one place they can hide from Sister

27

and still pretend to be busy if she catches them,' but didn't, because she had the distinct impression that the Senior Registrar knew the answer perfectly well already. Instead she sniffed hard and wiped a tear away with the back of her hand. 'I don't know what you mean and I wasn't skulking.'

'Oh, really?' There was a veiled note of sarcasm in his voice as he came closer and prised the sheet she was clutching from her lifeless fingers. She stared at it and at him.

'Then precisely what were you doing?'

'I was . . . I was marking the sheets that are beyond repair. They have to be disposed of and replaced,' she wavered.

His gaze wandered over the pile of sodden sheets and a nerve twitched at the corner of his mouth. 'I hope you weren't thinking of using any of those on the patients' beds. Sister is likely to think half the ward has suddenly become incontinent.'

In spite of herself she giggled. It was a mistake, she knew it as his expression froze. 'I see nothing even slightly humorous in this situation, Nurse, but possibly it was foolish of me to imagine that you might feel even the slightest remorse for your disgraceful conduct out there.'

She bit her lip, her fingers closing over the marking pen, stabbing the top furiously on and off as tears welled up again. It was so unfair. 'It . . . it wasn't like that. You don't understand. It was a joke and you weren't supposed to hear.'

'Then you badly underestimated me, Nurse, and I assure you it isn't wise to do that in anything. As for this "joke",' his mouth curled contemptuously, 'it was in exceedingly poor taste, or am I to take it that you make a habit of leaping into strange beds. patients' or otherwise?'

Her cheeks blazed crimson with humiliation. 'No, of course I don't.'

'That isn't the impression you give,' he thundered. 'Or perhaps the whole thing was simply an indication of how lightly you treat your work.'

Her brown eyes widened with horror as she stared at him. 'But that isn't true. I love my job.' She gulped hard and stared beyond him to the door. 'I suppose Sister is furious.'

His lips tightened and he was standing so close that suddenly she was aware of the faint lines of tiredness around his eyes and mouth. Such a fascinating mouth, even when he was angry. A pulse hammered in her throat.

'I think she has every right to be, don't you, Nurse?'

She nodded, too miserable to speak and felt a tear trickle coldly down her chin. 'I suppose I shall be asked to leave.'

'Oh, come on now, it's hardly that bad.'

'But it is. You don't understand.'

'Obviously not, but I'm beginning to realise there is an awful lot I don't understand about you, Nurse Benedict.' A nerve pulsed in his jaw as he frowned disdainfully at the crumpled hanky she was kneading between her fingers and with a muttered oath he proffered his own. 'For heaven's sake, use this and stop crying. Just because I had to deliver a much-deserved lecture doesn't mean it's the end of the world.'

She caught the faintly tantalising smell of aftershave as she took the handkerchief and blew hard.

It seemed a pity to spoil the pristine whiteness but he was standing over her. 'No, but it might as well be,' she said in a strangled voice. 'It—it doesn't matter how hard I try, I always make such a terrible mess of things and I really don't know why. S— Sister said I'm a disruptive influence and if it happened again I'd have to go.' She stared vaguely as red ink from the marking pen spread delicately across the white square and thrust the hanky behind her apron. 'It's not as if I *intend* losing patients,' she hiccuped. 'Or—or letting swing doors open on people.' She couldn't bring herself to look at him as she heard his muffled exclamation. She couldn't blame him for being furious. If only she could stop crying, but knowing that he was standing there looking at her with those steel-cold eyes only made things worse. 'And I really was only joking . . . about jumping into bed with Mr Hackett.'

'I didn't seriously imagine for one moment that you weren't.' He sounded vaguely annoyed.

'Y—you didn't?'

His hands were suddenly gripping her shoulders and his mouth was compressed into a tight line. 'Are you really so naïve that it hasn't occurred to you that some men may not treat such comments as a joke, you little idiot. You're not safe to be let out alone.'

Her teeth practically rattled as he shook her furiously and to her horror she burst into fresh tears. She heard him swear softly under his breath and suddenly her head was against his chest. She could hear his heart beating almost as fast as her own and the smell of his aftershave was there again and without knowing quite how it happened she heard him groan and his mouth came down firmly on her own unresisting one.

After the initial moment of shock her frozen limbs seemed to melt. If this was meant to be a punishment then it was the most exquisite form of torture ever devised, she thought incoherently. His hands moved to her face, drawing her relentlessly closer, brushing against her hair, loosening the pins, and went on remorselessly, inviting responses which her body gave until she moaned softly. It was utter madness but he seemed to have robbed her of the power to resist. She tasted the salt of her tears on her lips as she struggled with emotions so utterly sensuous that she could hardly breathe. It was all a dream of course, she told herself, but a dream she wanted to go on for ever.

The spell was shattered as she found herself suddenly thrust away to stand shaking with confusion. Her hand flew to her mouth where the pressure of his lips still remained and she felt the heat of her burning cheeks. But as she looked at him she heard him make an odd sound in his throat and his expression changed. Her gaze followed his to look with rapt and horrified fascination at the bizarre tracery drawn in brilliant scarlet across the once crisp whiteness of his coat and she heard the groan which escaped her own lips. It couldn't be. It wasn't possible. Feeling sick with dismay she stared down at the marking pen clutched tightly in her hand and shook her head, making incoherent sounds as she tried to explain.

'*Don't.*' His voice was icy. He seemed to be having difficulty speaking at all. 'Just don't say a word.'

She had the distinct feeling that if she tried he would cheerfully strangle her with those hands which only seconds ago had made her shiver with delight.

The door fell open beneath the force of Sister Meredith's hand and Emma felt herself shudder as in one single sweep the cold glance took in the scene—Emma's stricken face and the Senior Registrar who appeared to be suffering some kind of apoplectic fit. Sister's eyebrows were suddenly affected by some nervous tic as her mouth opened and closed and her gaze rested icily upon Emma who was suddenly all too well aware that her cap was crooked and her face flushed.

'I will see you in my office in fifteen minutes, Nurse.' Her voice banished even the consideration of an appeal. Dumb with terror Emma flung a desperate glance in Garrard Blair's direction but he was already at the door, Sister marching in his wake like a battleship prepared for war.

'My office is free, Mr Blair, if you wish to change your coat. I will send one of my nurses to fetch a clean one.'

Frozen to the spot Emma watched as he held the door for Sister to walk through, and heard his voice sounding ludicrously calm, so calm in fact that she blinked hard. 'Thank you, Sister, I'd be most grateful,' he glanced at his watch. 'And perhaps, since I have a few minutes to spare before I have to start my clinic, we could have that cup of tea after all.'

Sister's smile was a miracle to behold, Emma thought, watching the doors swing to a close before straightening her cap and heading for the kitchens to sluice cold water on to her burning cheeks.

Unfortunately, by the time she had her interview it was unlikely there would be any trace of it left. Sighing deeply she returned to the ward and studiously avoided Mr Hackett's conspiratorial little winks and chuckles every time she passed his bed.

CHAPTER FOUR

THE mid-morning drinks trolley was just being wheeled on to the ward as Emma saw the white-coated figure leave. He stood aside to let it pass, spoke briefly with Staff Nurse Blake and was gone, leaving Emma to rub her sweating palms against her apron before tapping on Sister's office door. Her mouth felt dry and it seemed an eternity before the summons to enter came.

When it did she crept into the glass-partitioned room and stood with hands clasped behind her, staring fixedly at the tray of empty cups and a plate of biscuits. Her stomach rumbled noisily. And the condemned man ate a hearty meal, she thought, in a burst of witty hysteria, smothering the thought as Sister's gaze rose.

'You sent for me, Sister.'

Laura Meredith's frowning gaze rose. 'Oh yes, Nurse Benedict.' She pushed a file across the desk. 'I want you to take this down to Records for me. Mr Simpson was discharged at the weekend but for some reason the file wasn't sent down and they will need it for his Outpatients appointment.'

'Yes, Sister.'

Emma unclenched her fingers sufficiently to take the file and waited. There had to be more. There was. Sister's fingers drummed ominously on the desk. 'Will you also go to X-ray and find out what

34

has happened to Mr Fawley's plates. Tell them that Mr Blair's registrar will need them for this afternoon's round.'

'Yes, Sister. Er . . . was that all, Sister?'

The iron-grey head rose, sharply, from the report she was writing. She had a headache and not even ten minutes in the Senior Registrar's charming company had moved it. 'Should there be anything else, Nurse?' she asked testily, and Emma felt herself go weak with disbelief.

'Oh, no, Sister, that is . . . I thought . . . Mr Blair . . .'

'Ah yes, Mr Blair. In future when he is on this ward you will remain quiet and preferably out of sight, Nurse. He is an extremely busy man. Far too busy to be distracted by nurses indulging in childish jokes. It is not the kind of behaviour I wish to see on my ward, do you understand, Nurse?'

'Yes, Sister.' Emma lowered her head.

'Then please make sure it doesn't happen again. And now,' she sighed deeply, 'I have a great deal to do and Nurse Richards could do with some help in giving the patients their drinks. Please hurry down to X-ray and get back as quickly as you can.' The telephone shrilled. Her hand lifted the receiver, cutting off the sound. 'Pasteur Ward. Speaking. No, no you want Men's Medical, Florence Ward, this is Men's Surgical. If you hold on I'll ask the switchboard to transfer the call.'

Emma stood listening and waiting. Was that it then? She wasn't to be sacked, or even reprimanded? Sister glared and she scuttled out of the office, flying down the stairs towards X-ray as if her feet had suddenly developed wings. She didn't understand what had happened but she knew better than to question it. There was no accounting for Sister's moods and perhaps the Senior Registrar had decided she was too unimportant after all. For some reason the thought banished her happiness. In fact he had probably already forgotten her. After all, that kiss could hardly have meant anything. Senior Registrars didn't know that first-year students existed. He had simply tried to comfort her, she told herself firmly. Except that it hadn't been comfort she had felt at all in his arms. Quite the contrary, her emotions had been roused in a way she hadn't dreamed possible, and her cheeks blazed so scarlet at the memory that Staff Nurse Blake paused to ask with some concern, 'Are you all right, Benedict? You look very flushed. Not going in for the 'flu are you?'

'Oh no, Staff. I'm fine, thank you,' Emma stammered, lowering her head purposefully over the jug of hot milk. 'It must be because I ran upstairs from X-ray.'

Staff Nurse Blake accepted the explanation with the merest frown. 'Nurses do not run, Nurse, except in dire emergencies.'

'No, Staff.'

Helen Blake walked briskly down the ward, her slim figure attractive in the neat, mauve uniform, blonde hair firmly in place beneath the frilled cap. Emma sighed with quiet envy.

Milk drinks dispensed to those patients who were allowed to have them, the trolley was wheeled away and those patients who weren't due for operations or who were recovering from them settled to read newspapers or wandered in dressing-gowns along to the day-room. To them it was a quiet lull in the midst of a boring day. To the staff it passed virtually unnoticed as the routine of the ward continued inexorably towards lunch time, visiting time, consultants' rounds and more visitors.

Sue Harper breezed into the kitchen with the tray from Sister's office. 'Gosh, my feet are killing me and we're not even half-way through the day yet. It's like being on a treadmill. Come on, Benedict, buck up. Sister's gone to a meeting and Staff's on the war-path.'

'Oh no, not again. How many pairs of hands does she think we have?' She filled the last of the plastic water jugs and wiped her hands. 'I'd better get these back to the ward.'

'Well, I'm just off for my coffee break. Mr Warner's due for theatre in half an hour and I'm taking him down.'

They sped in opposite directions as Staff rapped fiercely on the window. Emma hurriedly distributed a jug to each of the twenty-six lockers and was just congratulating herself on having achieved it in record time when she saw Staff Nurse Blake beckoning her from the office.

Helen Blake was ruefully studying the day's operating list and scarcely looked up as Emma presented herself.

'Yes, Staff?'

'I'm afraid the theatre list is going to have to be completely rescheduled, Nurse. I've just had a call to say an emergency is on its way in, a road accident I gather, so he'll have to be dealt with straight away.' She frowned. 'It means everyone will have to be put back. It's an awful nuisance but it can't be helped.'

'What about Mr Warner, Staff? He's on his way now.'

'That's all right, he's to go as planned. Theatre Two will take him, thank goodness. The poor man was so nervous. I hate this sort of thing but there's not a thing we can do about it.'

'No, Staff.'

'Nurse Harper isn't back from coffee yet is she?'

'Yes, Staff, she's taken Mr Warner up to theatre.'

'Oh yes, of course, well then I want you to get the empty bed ready. Male Nurse Richards can give you a hand. We don't know when the emergency will arrive but at least we can be prepared. Oh, and we shall need a Kardex making out as soon as any of the details are through.'

'Yes, Staff.'

'Off you go then, Benedict. I must go and explain to the rest of the patients on the list that they won't be getting their pre-meds until later.' She looked at her fob watch. 'By the way, what time are you due to go for lunch?'

'At one, Staff.'

'Right, don't hang about then.'

It was just as the lunches were being given out that the emergency arrived from theatre. Handing out portions of cauliflower cheese, Emma caught a brief glimpse of a very young white face as the trolley was wheeled by, then the curtains were drawn round the bed and she found herself faced with the inevitable questions.

'Don't look so good does 'e, Nurse?' Mr Hackett stared with vague horror at his plate. 'Can't say this does either.' He probed the mixture with a fork and sniffed disdainfully. 'Gawd, are you sure they ain't just wheeled this up from theatre too? It don't look as if it made it.'

Emma pursed her lips primly. 'Now, Mr Hackett, that is good, nourishing food. You eat it, it will do you good.'

'I ain't so sure. It might set me back weeks.'

'Mr Hackett, *I* will set you back weeks if you don't behave. The meals served in this hospital are all perfectly nutritionally balanced and, as a matter of fact, the standards of cooking are extremely high, I will have you know.'

'Cor,' he grinned up at her. 'Go on, you're lovely when you're in a temper. Give us a kiss.'

She evaded his out-thrust hands. 'Mr Hackett, please. Do you want to get me into trouble with Sister?'

He chuckled. 'She's only jealous.'

'Oh, really.' She tried to be cross but somehow a giggle escaped her, only to die as she became aware of the tall figure glancing coldly in her direction as he strode down the centre of the ward.

Her heart missed a beat as she bent furiously to straighten the corners of the counterpane, only to find Mr Hackett clutching at her arm.

''Ere, what's up with 'im then, Nurse?'

''Im . . . er, him, Mr Hackett?' she said, flustered, as the colour rose in her cheeks.

The fork stabbed in the direction of the curtained bed. ''E didn't look too good.'

She breathed a sigh of relief and said briskly, 'I've really no idea. He was admitted as an emergency and went straight to theatre. We've had no details yet and in any case I'm sure you don't seriously expect me to discuss another patient.'

Mr Hackett was voicing his disappointment when Emma caught Sister's eye. 'Nurse Benedict, please get these lunches served and out of the way. I want this ward cleared and tidied thoroughly before Dr Singh does his round this afternoon.' Sister glanced at her watch. 'When you've finished you can go to lunch and don't be late back. We're in for a busy afternoon and I shall need everyone to pull their weight.'

'No, Sister.' With a grimace she hurried back to the trolley, ladling cauliflower cheese on to plates for Mike Richards to hand out. 'I know one thing,' she muttered fervently, 'if it's cauliflower cheese for lunch I shall be starving by tonight. I can't stand the stuff.'

Fixing a smile on her face she approached one of the beds. 'Here we are, Mr Langley. Eat it all up or Sister will want to know why.'

'Thank you, Nurse,' a voice murmured coolly from behind her, and she spun round to face Sister Meredith's frosty gaze. 'Go to lunch *now*, please, and don't take all day about it.'

'Yes, Sister. No, Sister—three bags full, Sister,' she added under her breath as she headed for the doors and down the stairs to the staff cafeteria.

CHAPTER FIVE

THE cafeteria was crowded and noisy as Emma took her place in the queue, looking for an empty table and knowing full well that there wasn't likely to be one. She stood with her plate of roast beef and two veg and was heading for the coffee when she saw Sally Faulkener waving frantically from across the room, and she hurried in that direction with enormous relief.

She put her tray down, disgorging plate, cutlery and coffee on to the table before sliding into the seat. 'Thank goodness. I was just beginning to think I'd have to eat standing up.'

'I knew you'd be down so I kept a place.' Sally pushed salt and pepper towards her and drained her own cup of coffee. 'I've got to get back in a few minutes. We're rushed off our feet and we're busy trying to organise a farewell do for Sister without her knowing anything about it. You remember Sister Kilairn? She used to be Stevens before she married Mr Kilairn the consultant.'

Emma's fork hovered half-way to her mouth. 'Oh yes, she was on the first ward I went to from PTS, only she was a Staff Nurse then. She got her promotion when Sister Jacobs left.'

'That's right, well she's expecting a baby.'

'No.' Emma's eyes widened. 'But that's super.' Her nose prickled with emotion. 'I love babies. I wouldn't mind four. The trouble is, I'm not likely to find a dishy consultant who'll take me on. Some people have all the luck.' She sighed wistfully.

'I know what you mean. Oh well, we'll just have to set our sights a bit lower. Talking of which, are you going to the do next weekend?'

'Do?'

'Yes, you know, to celebrate the finals.'

Emma shifted uncomfortably. 'As a matter of fact I thought I might pop over to see my family. It's been ages . . .' she probed a layer of beef with her knife. 'I suppose you're going?'

'But of course. Tony Rowlands asked me weeks ago. Honestly, you can't not go. I mean, one of these days it's going to be our turn.'

'Hm, yours maybe.' Emma chewed disconsolately. 'Anyway, the truth is I really don't fancy turning up on my own.'

'Well what about Mike Richards?'

'He hasn't actually asked me, and even if he had,' she added, quickly, seeing her friend's sharp look, 'I'm really not keen on that sort of thing. All those housemen.'

'Mm, lovely. I'm hoping I might come across one who's so stoned he won't remember that he didn't ask me to marry him.'

Emma grinned and took the words with a pinch of salt. Sally was a pretty girl who had men queueing up to take her out, unlike some, she thought, munching her way stoically through thick potato.

The cafeteria was clearing gradually as most of the staff on early lunch made their way back to various departments and Sally sped away to Women's Surgical. Sitting back with her coffee,

Emma studied the small groups who lingered and found her gaze drawn to a couple who sat apparently arguing, if the girl's tear-stained face was anything to go by. She recognised her, vaguely, as a first-year from Casualty and the grim-faced young man as Phil Carrington, a junior houseman with a reputation for collecting attractive nurses.

Studying the tall, blond good looks Emma could understand why, and felt her own heart miss a beat before she looked away and began to stir her coffee vigorously.

She wondered why the girl with him was looking so miserable when practically every nurse at St Clement's was just waiting for Phil Carrington to raise his hand and beckon.

It was some seconds before she realised that her stare was being returned by a stunningly vivid pair of masculine blue eyes and her cheeks flamed hotly. For a second a frown marred the handsome features before he turned away, and she saw the girl say something crossly as she glanced, briefly, in her direction. Emma stared hurriedly down at her coffee and gulped it down far too quickly for comfort. The staff cafeteria was hardly a comfortable place to have a lovers' tiff.

Envy faded and she felt a momentary surge of pity for the white-faced girl who was probably in for a miserable afternoon.

She yawned and stretched and was just summoning the energy to go back to Men's Surgical when she heard raised voices and without intending it, found her gaze drawn back to the other table. She saw the girl thrust back her chair and say something sharply before running, weeping, from the now near-empty cafeteria. Phil Carrington was on his feet, his face grim as he looked after the retreating figure. True love obviously wasn't running smoothly.

Feeling like an intruder, Emma toyed with the idea of waiting until he had gone before making her way past his table and back to the ward, but he seemed in no hurry to move and she had about five minutes to make the stairs and tidy her hair before Sister saw her.

This is ridiculous, she told herself, averting her gaze as she headed for the door. If people argued in public places they must expect to be seen and overheard. She hadn't intended eavesdropping so why should the sight of his tense features make her feel guilty?

His gaze rose, angrily, as she drew level with the table where he was sitting hunched over a half-empty cup of coffee. For a moment she thought she was going to be allowed to pass when his gaze fixed itself more firmly on her face and she felt herself blush as he stared at her, frowning in vague recognition. As if coming to a sudden decision he got to his feet, effectively barring her path.

'Hullo, I know you don't I?'

Startled she looked at him and blinked. 'N—no, I don't think so.' It was hardly likely, she thought. I'm strictly not his type. If only I were. Her heart fluttered as he smiled.

'Hm, funny. I could have sworn . . . but you see so many faces in passing in a place like this.' His gaze seemed to be taking in each of her features in detail and the spot on her chin suddenly throbbed and seemed ten times larger than when she had first looked at it that morning. The smile flashed devastatingly again. 'Some I remember better than others. Yours was obviously one that stuck in my mind.'

She giggled nervously, and he moved aside, saying casually, as if totally unaware of the effect he was having on her, 'Perhaps it was on Casualty.'

Her mouth unfroze. 'No, I don't think so. Actually I'm on Men's Surgical. But I do get down to Casualty once in a while, when sent on an errand of mercy, so to speak.' She was sure he hadn't a clue what she was babbling about.

'Well, that's it then.' He smiled directly at her. 'I knew I couldn't forget beautiful brown velvet eyes like those.'

Emma felt her breath catch in her throat, painfully aware of the effect he was having on her heartbeat. The swing doors loomed ahead. She wanted to walk backwards, knowing that the instant they walked through them he would walk away and dismiss her completely from his mind. But he didn't. Instead he swung round to face her, one hand pressed against the wall where she stood. Dimly she was aware of the curious glances being cast in their direction and wondered what the hospital grapevine would make of this. St Clement's most eligible, good looking doctor, talking to *her*. She bit her lip and pretended she hadn't noticed the glances. He had such beautiful eyes, especially when they smouldered as they were at this moment with what she hoped, breathlessly, might be passion.

'I'm sorry you had to witness that bloody little scene. I suppose you must have heard?'

She fought her disappointment. So it hadn't been passion after all. 'Well . . . actually I . . .'

'My dear girl,' he brushed aside her hesitation. 'I'm sorry, take no notice. I've no right to burden you with my problems. It's just that I find it hard to know how to deal with jealous tantrums.' His mouth was grim and beautiful too. 'Especially when they are totally unfounded.' He gave a lop-sided grin. 'But there we are, I suppose that's the penalty you pay when you have a reputation—even when it's undeserved.'

Emma's heartbeat quickened in defence. 'Oh, but I'm sure it isn't . . .'

'Undeserved?'

She coloured to her most awful shade of beet-root. 'Oh no, really, I didn't mean . . . well I meant . . . it doesn't seem fair, that's all,' she finished lamely and his eyebrows rose.

'What's this? Have I a champion? And such a fierce little one too.' He had moved closer and she had to stop herself from leaping a foot in the air as his finger suddenly stroked her cheek. 'Well, I'm flattered. What did you say your name was, little mouse?'

'B—Benedict. Emma Benedict.' A tingling sensation was making its way down her spine.

'Ah yes, of course.' His smile teased gently. 'Well, I shan't forget you, Emma Benedict. In fact I'm beginning to think you might be good for me. A refreshing change.' His lips brushed lightly against her mouth and she felt her knees turn to jelly. 'I suppose you'll be going to this awful do next week, along with the rest of the herd?'

Propping herself against the wall so that she

wouldn't buckle at the knees completely, she gazed up at him and heard herself say, with a naïvety which made her want to kick herself, 'No, actually I don't have anyone to go with.'

'Well, well,' he drawled softly, 'perhaps we may be able to remedy that.' He stared at her for a moment, then straightened up, frowning as he glanced at his watch. 'Damn, I'm going to get a rocket if I don't get down to Casualty straight away. I should have been there five minutes ago.'

Emma came down to earth with a bump. Her own gaze flew in horror to the clock on the wall. 'Oh no, and I should be back on Men's Surgical.'

She was flying down the corridor, dragging her cap back into place when she realised that he hadn't actually asked her to go with him after all. She flew in through the swing doors, kept a wary eye out for Sister and stood gasping for breath. 'Oh well,' she sighed miserably, 'it was nice while it lasted, even if it was only ten seconds. I should have known better than to imagine a man like Phil Carrington would actually look at me. After all, why pick a weed when you can have the pick of the bunch!'

CHAPTER SIX

THE ward was filled with September sunshine as the first of the afternoon's visitors began to arrive and stand impatiently in the corridor outside the ward.

'Right, Nurse.' Staff nodded in Emma's direction. 'You can let them in, and see to the flowers will you? We're getting a bit short of vases and judging from that lot,' she eyed the bunches of chrysanthemums and roses, 'we're going to need some, so you'd better shoot over to Lister and borrow a few.'

'Yes, Staff.' Emma leapt back as the doors flew open and visitors surged into the ward, bringing heady wafts of flowers and a sudden shattering of calm.

For the next two hours she was kept busy bustling in and out of the kitchen, arranging flowers and providing fruit bowls, and she threw a conspiratorial glance in Fred Hackett's direction as he handed her the inevitable bunch of grapes, whilst generally answering visitors' queries.

'Yes, visiting is from two until four every afternoon, except Mondays which is our busiest operating day. Oh no, Mrs Langley, your husband decided to watch television. You'll find him in the lounge.'

She smiled at the irate lady who muttered darkly under her breath, 'Just the same at home. Never know where he is from one minute to the next. Can't you keep him in bed, Nurse?'

Emma glanced hopefully at Staff Blake who paused briefly to smile. 'I'm afraid we can't do that, Mrs Langley. We don't believe in keeping patients in bed. It's far better for them to be up and about as soon as possible, isn't it, Nurse?'

'Yes, definitely, Staff.' Emma confirmed decisively, but Staff was already moving briskly down the ward, pausing occasionally to chat with patients and visitors.

'I could do with a few days in bed myself,' Mrs Langley retorted, easing up a large carrier bag and carrying it and her aching varicose veins in search of her husband. 'I never knew a man yet who wasn't dying the minute he sneezed.'

Emma grimaced at Mike Richards and shot into the kitchens as Sister's eye wavered in her direction. 'All right, I'm going, I'm going,' she hissed under her breath and began to prepare afternoon tea and slices of bread and butter and fruit cake.

It was part of the job she always enjoyed, taking the tea trolley round, handing out the cups and being able to exchange a few words with the visitors. There was only one at the bed of the patient who had been admitted after the road accident. A young girl who sat in tearful silence behind the drawn curtains which shut her off from the rest of the ward.

Emma popped her head round, holding a cup of tea in her hand. The girl nodded, a fleeting smile appearing on her lips. Her hands shook as Emma gave her the cup and she said in a hesitant whisper, 'He's going to be all right isn't he, Nurse? I mean, he looks so awful lying there like that.'

Emma looked at the sleeping man whose head was bandaged and who had one arm and both legs in plaster. 'I know everyone is doing their best,' she murmured noncommittally. It was part of their training that they never made guesses or offered opinions upon a patient's medical condition. Doctors alone were qualified to do that and in Jim Squires' case it was still very early days. 'Have you spoken to Sister? I'm sure she'll be happy to answer any questions you might have.'

The girl's worried gaze rose reluctantly from the sleeping man to Emma. 'I don't really like to. Can't you tell me how bad he is? You know all about these things, don't you, after all you're a trained nurse.'

For a moment Emma's heart lifted. Someone actually had confidence in her, but then a great many visitors simply assumed that any uniform signified a fully-qualified nurse. She straightened up, ruefully indicating her name badge. 'I'm sorry, I'm only a first-year student. You'd be better talking to Staff or Sister, and they may even be able to arrange for you to see the doctor.' She glanced at the girl's left hand. 'You're not married, to the patient, I mean?'

To her dismay the girl's eyes filled with tears. 'No. We were going to be, in a month's time. Only now . . .' she began to sob quietly and Emma rested a hand on her shoulder.

'Come on, cheer up. A month's a long time and Mr Squires is a fighter. Well you can't blame him, can you, with so much to look forward to. It might be a blessing in a way.'

The girl smiled, hopefully, through her tears. 'Yes, it might, mightn't it? It may just mean postponing the date for a few weeks. Perhaps you're right, I will speak to Sister.'

Emma went back to the tea trolley, finished handing out the tea and cake, and went in search of Sister. 'Oh Sister, the young lady with Mr Squires was asking me about his progress and I suggested she might have a chat to you. I hope that's all right?'

Sister nodded approvingly. 'Yes, of course, Nurse.' She reached for the Kardex, frowning. 'She isn't his wife. I see he isn't married.'

'No, Sister. I gather they are engaged and were to be married in a month's time. I think . . . well I think she wants to know . . .'

Sister Meredith sighed. 'Yesterday I'd have said his chances of walking anywhere, let alone down the aisle, were practically nil. Today I'd say they are marginally better, but certainly not in a month's time, and I wouldn't care to put any time limit on it. He has a serious skull fracture and those legs were pretty badly smashed, but if he's a determined young man, who's to say?' She looked at her watch. 'I'll see her after visiting is over, Nurse. Or if Mr Squires is sleeping I can have a chat with her now.'

'Thank you, Sister. I'll tell her.'

The rest of the afternoon flew by. Emma cleared the afternoon tea things away before going for her own coffee break.

Without meaning to she found herself looking for Phil Carrington, even though she knew he wasn't likely to be there. She returned to the ward feeling faintly disgruntled, in time to be caught by Staff Nurse Blake and to notice that a certain amount of activity was going on behind the curtains drawn round Jim Squires' bed. A quick spasm of alarm passed through her as she saw Dr Singh emerge, his shiny dark features unsmiling as he walked down the ward beside Sister.

Emma caught Mike as he was carrying a bedpan to the sluice. 'What's going on?'

'It's Mr Squires. They're not happy about him. I think he suddenly took a slight turn for the worse.'

'Oh no.'

'Singh's just been in to see him. I think they're considering moving him into a side-ward or up to Intensive Care.'

Emma stared bleakly at him, her throat suddenly felt very tight. 'He was hoping to get married soon.'

'Well, he may still,' Mike looked at her, gently. 'You have to look on the bright side, you know, and try not to let it get you down.'

'I do try but it isn't easy.'

'Of course it isn't. If you didn't care you wouldn't be human, and if you weren't human you wouldn't make a good nurse. Sometimes you just have to shut yourself off from the more depressing side of it that's all, otherwise you'd never survive.'

She nodded, clamped her lips together and went back to the ward. Mike was right, but what he had said only made her all the more certain that she would never be a first-class nurse.

There was about an hour to go before she went off-duty and she stared with sudden depression at the rain pouring down the windows.

'How on earth can it change so quickly?' she demanded, peevishly.

Sue Harper grimaced sympathetically. 'I suppose we'll have to make a dash for it. At least it isn't far to the Nurses' Home and it may have stopped by the time we go off. What are you doing for tea by the way? Going to the cafeteria?'

'No, I don't think so. This is definitely a toast-and-jam-by-the-fire night.'

'Mm, sounds lovely.'

'Well come over and join me, then. I don't particularly fancy my own company. Just give me half an hour to bath and change into something fairly civilised. I may even be in a better mood.'

'I'll do that. It will give me a chance to write a letter anyway, and not before time, as my mother keeps reminding me.' She launched herself energetically behind the medicine trolley and Emma skipped through the doors and headed for the X-ray department, clutching the file Staff had asked her to return. She was so lost in thought that she didn't see the hurrying figure advancing behind her until a hand closed on her arm. She jumped, turned and found herself staring up into Phil's smiling features.

'I thought it was you. I was afraid you'd disappear before I could catch you.'

Her heart was doing crazy things again. The thought that he should want to catch her sent an odd little quiver down her spine.

'I was just on my way to X-ray before I go off duty and across to the Nurses' Home.'

He raised an amused eyebrow and leaned closer. 'I'll bet they pull up the drawbridge at midnight and post sentries on all the doors.'

She giggled nervously. 'It's not quite that bad. We're not living in the Middle Ages, you know.'

'I'll take your word for it,' he murmured huskily. 'My God, you really have got beautiful eyes.'

She blushed furiously, and opened them even wider. 'Anyway, it's just that they like us to be in at a reasonable hour, for our own sakes as much as everyone else's.' She didn't know why she was bothering to explain. He probably knew as much about the rules as she did. Not that she imagined Phil Carrington was a man who abided by them unless it suited him.

She looked away quickly, realising he was teasing. 'I'd better go. I have to get back to the ward.'

'And then what? A date I suppose?' Suddenly he wasn't smiling.

She wished he hadn't asked. 'No,' she laughed. 'As a matter of fact I've promised to make toast for tea. Not very exciting is it?'

'It sounds very cosy. Perhaps I shall be honoured with an invitation one day, or are men strictly taboo within those hallowed cloisters?'

Emma blushed. She was never quite sure when he was being serious, but there was a kind of wistful appeal in his eyes as he stared at her.

'No, of course they're not. But I . . . well, I don't imagine you'd find toast and jam very exciting somehow.'

'My dear infant, don't judge me by the hospital grapevine. My character has been greatly maligned.'

'Oh . . . yes, I'm sure it has.'

'Good, then as long as that's understood you'll feel quite happy about accepting my invitation.'

She blinked hard, wondering if she had missed something. 'Invitation?'

'To the do next week of course.' The doors behind him opened and he drew her to one side, letting two young housemen pass. Their glances slid over her, then she saw them grin as Phil raised a hand and muttered something she didn't quite catch before they disappeared along the corridor.

It was some seconds before she realised that Phil's arm had slipped round her waist and that his hand was tracing the curve of her breast. She detached herself from his grasp, primly smoothing her uniform and hoping her voice sounded casual instead of breathless as she was sure it must. 'The do?'

'You're not going with someone else after all, are you?' He said it with a terseness which took her by surprise.

'No . . . oh no. It's just that I imagined you would be, I mean . . . Nurse Collins . . .' She gulped hard, wishing she hadn't conjured up the tear-stained face of the girl. 'I'm sure you'd much rather. I know you've had a tiff, but I'm sure you could talk it over and make up.'

His face had hardened and lost some of its niceness. 'My dear girl, I've no intention of "making up" as you put it, especially for something which wasn't my fault. I'm asking *you*. Are you trying to tell me you don't want to go, or just that you don't want to go with me in particular?'

'Oh no.' Dear God, now she had offended him and he would never ask her again. 'It's just that I thought . . . well, I mean, there are so many attractive nurses who would just fall over themselves . . .'

He laughed softly and his lips brushed disconcertingly over hers. 'A man can get awfully tired of stepping over attractive females.' He was nibbling at her ear. 'There's a freshness about you, Emma Benedict. You're a challenge and I can't resist challenges. You're not going to disappoint me, are you?'

Weakly she heard herself deny it, then, with an abruptness which left her feeling bewildered, he kissed her and set her free.

'Good girl, I knew I could count on you.'

She was still besottedly trying to convince herself that this wasn't all a dream when the doors swung open again and a white-coated figure strode past. Emma wondered why the steel-dark eyes fixed themselves upon her face with such ferocity, then her heart contracted as the Senior Registrar's gaze slid coldly over Phil.

'Aren't you supposed to be in Casualty, Carrington? I understood it was part of your job to put in an appearance occasionally. When you can spare the time, of course. We wouldn't wish to overburden you.'

Emma was aware of Phil stiffening beside her and was feeling a surge of defensive pity when he said sheepishly, 'Yes, sir. As a matter of fact I was just on my way there now.' He was gone without a backward glance and Emma felt her knees quake as the ice-cold gaze returned to her own face.

From beneath lowered lashes she stole a look at him. He must recognise her, she thought, waiting for the axe to fall. But if he did there was no sign of it in the coldly autocratic gaze.

'Aren't you supposed to be on duty, Nurse? If so I suggest you get back to your ward instead of loitering in corridors making assignations with members of my staff.'

She gasped, a furious retort rising to her lips only to be silenced as he strode away without even giving her a chance to defend herself. Not, she thought miserably, as she returned to the ward, that she could have denied it anyway. Even so, he needn't have been so thoroughly overbearing to poor Phil.

She reached the ward and was summoned immediately by Staff Nurse Blake. 'Oh, there you are, Nurse. Mr Harris is just back from theatre. The usual checks will need to be done. In this case there is a drain *in situ* as well, so you'd better come along with me and give a hand. It's the best way of getting to know what is happening.' She moved to the bedside and smiled down at the still very drowsy figure.

'Hullo, Mr Harris, how are you feeling?'

Emma watched as Helen Blake's attractively long fingers went to the man's wrist and she checked his pulse. The man's eyes fluttered open, revealing the confusion of a patient still coming round after an operation.

'What time is it?'

Staff smiled. 'It's half-past four, Mr Harris.' He looked bemused. 'You've had your operation and you're back on the ward. Everything is fine so go back to sleep again.' He obeyed, as if the sound of a familiar voice was all the reassurance he had needed and Staff smiled again. 'It's funny how many of them want to know what time it is, although I suppose it's fairly understandable.' She filled in the chart at the end of the bed and nodded at Emma. 'You check his blood pressure, Nurse, and I'll have a look at the drain. You know what the drain is, of course?'

'Yes, Staff. It's a tube which is sometimes inserted after an abdominal operation in order to remove any discharge.'

'Very good.' Staff continued the routine checks, made the necessary observations on the chart and returned it to the clip at the foot of the bed. 'Mr Harris has come through his operation very well. He'll be drowsy for several hours yet but by tomorrow he'll be feeling much better and sitting up and taking notice.' She looked at her watch. 'I expect the House Surgeon will be round to see him shortly, just to check on his progress and make sure there aren't any signs of shock. You're off-duty in a few minutes aren't you?'

'Yes, Staff.'

'Fine, well scuttle round and make sure there aren't any newspapers lying around and all the water jugs are filled, then you can go.'

'Yes, Staff. Thank you, Staff.'

'What are you on tomorrow?'

'The same, Staff. Eight 'til five.'

'Right, well off you go then.' She was already bustling away when Emma went after her to ask,

'Sorry, Staff, but can you tell me how Mr Squires is? The young man who was brought in after the road accident.'

'He's not very well, I'm afraid. He's been moved up to Intensive Care but there's a possibility he may have to have another operation.' She frowned. 'It doesn't look too good, but obviously they are doing everything possible and he certainly couldn't be in better hands.'

'No, Staff.' Emma thought bleakly of his fiancée and wondered how she was feeling. Staff Nurse Blake's voice intruded sharply upon the thought.

'Go home, Nurse, and don't be late in the morning. It's Sister's day off and I shall be in charge, and we have a very full list.'

Emma went. It had been a long, hard day and she needed to get over it before thinking about tomorrow.

CHAPTER SEVEN

HAVING promised herself an early start, Emma stared accusingly at the silent alarm clock and raced to answer whoever was pounding on her door. She threw it open to find Sue, fully-dressed, regarding her anxiously.

'I thought so . . . That alarm of yours must have rung itself to a standstill. How on earth do you do it, Benedict? You'll have to get a move on if you're going to make it in time. I'm just off, I'll try and cover for you if I can.'

Emma groaned and made a dash for the bathroom, emerging from the Nurses' Home ten minutes later, still pink from a too-hot shower and wondering how on earth she was going to stave off the pangs of hunger until mid-morning coffee break.

She hurried through the large glass doors into Main Reception and immediately became aware of a familiar quickening to her pulse. There was something about the atmosphere of the old but famous hospital which seemed to grip her. Not just the light and airiness of its newly-modernised portals and wards, but the smell. She knew that a lot of people didn't like the faint but definite hint of antiseptic, the coldness of stainless steel and what the outsider often saw as the cold efficiency of a hospital at work, but she felt none of those things. On the contrary, she loved them, seeing them rather as a source of hope for the people who came through those doors sick and went out, most of them at least, cured.

Her chin rose and with a smile on her lips she answered the cheery wave of Harry, the small, stout figure behind the desk.

'Morning, Nurse.'

'Morning, Harry. Going to be busy today are we?'

Harry sniffed. 'Shouldn't be surprised, 'uman nature being what it is. Nothing new on your ward, though, so far. Quiet night in fact.'

'Oh well, that will have pleased Night Sister anyway,' Emma humoured him. Harry liked to give his own daily report, even if it was often interspersed with colourful detail and snippets of gossip. 'How's the cold, Harry?'

He knew better than to suspect little Nurse Benedict of being sarcastic. 'Tain't never goin' to get any better,' he sighed. 'Central 'eating it is what does it.'

'I'm sure you're right, Harry.' Keeping a wary eye on the clock she caught sight of Sally Faulkener waving to her from the door leading to the stairs. 'Any post for Men's Surgical, Harry? I may as well take it with me.'

'Aye, here we are.' He handed over a bundle and she sped away, catching up with her friend so that they trotted up the stairs together.

'Phew, I thought I wasn't going to make it, and all I need is to be late for report.'

'You've got three minutes.' Sally held the door open. 'I don't suppose you've had any more thoughts about going to the do have you? It would be nice to make up a foursome. Tony can always bring one of his friends along.'

Emma studied the pile of letters in her hands sheepishly. 'As a matter of fact I am going after all. Actually, Phil Carrington asked me.'

'Phil Carrington?'

There were times when Emma wished her friend's face wasn't quite so expressive. She bit her lip crossly, wondering why she should suddenly find herself on the defensive as Sally suddenly veered off into the cloakroom, dragging her with her. 'You're not serious?'

'Yes, of course I am.' Her mouth tightened. 'You're not going to start quoting the hospital grapevine at me, are you, because I know all about his reputation and I'm sure it's grossly exaggerated. Anyway, it's one date, not a lifetime's commitment.'

Sally was watching her with a wealth of pity in her eyes. 'I thought his present commitment was to Andrea Collins in Casualty.'

'Yes, well it was,' Emma felt her face turning pink, 'but they had a row and I probably caught him in a moment of weakness. Or,' she studied her face in the mirror, 'perhaps it's my hidden charms.' She closed in upon her reflection baring her teeth. 'Or could it be the new toothpaste?'

'Honestly, Benedict . . .' Sally gave a groan of exasperation. 'Well, I just hope you know what you're doing.'

'I don't suppose I do.' They headed out through the doors again. 'Still, if Cinders gets to go to the ball after all, she may as well enjoy it.'

Sally turned towards Men's Medical. 'Well at

least there's safety in numbers. Look, I'd better dash. I'll see you at lunch with any luck. We can talk about it then.' She dashed on to the ward and Emma made her way on to Men's Surgical, a smile on her lips as she felt the familiar routine of the ward close in around her.

Night Sister had departed and Staff Nurse Blake was going over the Kardex, discussing each patient's condition in turn and generally setting out the day's work. 'No new admissions,' she said crisply, 'which is just as well because heaven knows where we would have put them.'

'Grace Ward has a couple of empty beds, Staff,' Julie Stanton the third-year nurse said. Grace Ward was the other Male Surgical Ward.

Staff frowned. 'They're on take this weekend though, aren't they? Oh well, I dare say it will sort itself out. It usually does somehow.'

The pace of the day seemed to be set by the shrilling of the telephone bell. Staff leapt to answer it, leaving Julie Stanton to ensure that the daily routine was under way.

Beds were made, and the inevitable round of medicines; pulse, temperature and respiration checks; dressings, interspersed with mid-morning drinks, lunches and the comings and goings between the ward and theatre. Emma found she scarcely had time to think of anything beyond the task in hand. There were patients to be got ready for theatre and others coming back who needed constant and careful nursing.

'You can go to theatre with Mr Thornton, Nurse.' Staff caught Emma just as she finished sorting a pile of soiled linen. 'He's just had his pre-med so it should be taking effect fairly soon.'

'Yes, Staff.'

'Oh, and on your way back, pop into X-ray and see if they have managed to find Mr Warner's plates. Mr Blair is in theatre this morning so Dr Stevington will be doing his rounds and he's bound to want them.'

Emma's heart gave a light skip of relief at the thought that she wasn't going to bump into the Senior Registrar this morning at least. She liked his registrar, everyone did. Pete Stevington was young, good at this job and hadn't yet acquired the icy aloofness of his superior.

The theatre porters in their white coats and boots arrived to take Mr Thornton to theatre. Emma felt her hand gripped tightly as they wheeled the trolley down the ward and out through the swing doors towards the lift. She smiled in what she hoped was a reassuring manner. The pre-med was working and the look of fear had gone, leaving the patient drowsy and no longer caring about what was to happen. To Emma it was one of the miracles of modern medicine and she often found herself wondering what it must have been like to be a nurse in the days when things had been so much more primitive, when a patient like Mr Thornton would probably have faced his operation in far different conditions.

Swing doors opened and the trolley was man-oeuvred deftly through into an ante-room, beyond which more doors led into the strange world of the operating theatres. Emma glanced down at her patient. This was as far as she could go with him.

'You'll be given an injection in a moment, Mr Thornton, and you'll go off to sleep. When you wake up again the operation will all be over and you'll be back on the ward, and I shall come and tuck you in.'

He smiled drowsily, without opening his eyes. Theatre Sister approached, nodding dismissal. Emma sped away in the direction of the X-ray department.

Passing Casualty and Outpatients she looked hopefully for some sign of Phil but to no avail, which was probably as well, she told herself, because both departments were busy and even if she had seen him there wouldn't have been an opportunity to speak. She walked briskly past the rows of patients. Several looked up, hopefully, in her direction as she came towards them, only to settle back crossly again as she hurried past, smiling apologetically. She couldn't blame them. Despite an appointments system, the department was always so busy that doctors, nurses and receptionists alike were rushed off their feet.

X-ray was busy too, with patients in wheelchairs, patients in dressing-gowns and a heavily pregnant young woman all waiting for attention.

Collecting the X-rays she had been sent to find she returned to the ward where, after giving them a cursory glance, Staff inserted them with a flourish into the appropriate file on the trolley.

'Thank you, Nurse, now will you go and help Nurse Stanton with the dressings trolley, Dr Stevington will be here in five minutes. And later will you give Nurse Richards a hand to check sterile supplies. We're running a bit short.'

'Yes, Staff.'

It came as a shock some time later to hear Staff telling her to go to lunch. Glancing disbelievingly at the clock she obeyed, wondering where on earth the morning had gone.

Fortified by beef casserole and treacle pudding she returned as Staff Nurse Blake went off for her own lunch and found Nurse Stanton feverishly trying to round up the patients who were due for discharge.

'Look in the television room, Nurse, and tell Mr Slater that his transport will be here in ten minutes.'

Emma returned with the culprit and escorted him to the door of the ward, waving him off as he left with the hospital driver before going to have her last chat with Mr Hackett.

She found him prowling by the window, watching for the first influx of afternoon visitors. He looked different somehow, fully-dressed, but she supposed nurses felt about their patients pretty much as outsiders felt about nurses—that they all looked alike in uniform.

'Hullo, Mr Hackett, ready for the off then?'

He turned and grinned. 'Ar, can't wait to get 'ome to a decent cup of tea and me own bed.'

'Oh dear, are we really that bad?'

'Nah,' he chuckled, 'but it ain't the Ritz, is it?' His gaze slid in the direction of Sister's office. 'More like Gestapo headquarters.'

Emma giggled. 'For heaven's sake don't let anyone hear you say that. Anyway, it's not really that bad.'

''Course it's not. Not the same as yer own place though, is it? Mind you, I'll miss seeing you around.

Always 'ad time for a chat and a joke, not like some, and I appreciated that.' He pulled something from his pocket and thrust it at her, self-consciously. 'I thought you might like these, just by way of a thank you like.'

Emma felt herself blush as she took the box of chocolates and suddenly found herself struggling to speak. 'They're lovely, but there was really no need.'

'I know there weren't, all the same, I'm grateful.' He looked at her with doleful eyes and she felt her throat tighten as she said brightly, 'Well, I expect your daughter will be here in a few minutes to collect you. Have you been given a letter for your doctor, and you know the District Nurse will be out to see you shortly after you get home?'

'Yes, Staff Nurse told me.'

'Good.' She smiled. It was always hard saying goodbye to patients she had become particularly attached to. Nurses weren't supposed to, of course, but still it happened. Shaking his hand she walked quickly away and minutes later saw him leave, waving to him from the kitchen before she bent to the task of arranging yet more flowers and serving the afternoon tea.

Visiting was over. The empty beds were already filled by new patients looking edgy and self-conscious, and those who had come back from theatre all seemed to be progressing normally. Emma eased her aching back and followed Mike Richards into the sluice.

'Any news of Mr Squires?'

'Not much. He's still in Intensive Care, though I gather they've managed to relieve some of the pressure from the skull fracture which was worrying them.'

'Oh well, thank heavens for that. I feel so sorry for his fiancée.'

'Well don't start getting all dewy-eyed. He's a patient like all the rest you know. They all need an equal share of your attention, but not your emotions.'

'I know, I know.' She clamped her teeth together and followed him out on to the ward.

'Nurse Richards,' Staff beckoned. 'Mr Harris looks rather uncomfortable. Straighten his sheets and raise his pillows will you. Nurse Benedict give a hand.'

Emma stood at one side of the bed and Mike at the other as the patient was gently rolled to one side and the sheet pulled taut beneath him. Supporting him gently round the shoulders the pillows were plumped and rearranged and he settled back with a sigh.

'There we are, Mr Harris, how's that?'

'Much better thanks, Nurse. I don't know how it happens but I always seem to find myself sliding down the bed after a while.'

Mike grinned. 'It's hospital sheets. Special variety. Why do you think we have to learn to do such neat corners? It's to stop the patients sliding out.'

The man chuckled, then remembered his stitches and grinned. He was still grinning as Staff called Emma and she trotted obediently across the ward. 'Yes, Staff?'

Staff Nurse Blake's expression was one of resignation. 'Nurse, I find it hard to believe we issued you with a cap that shape.'

Emma's hands flew to her head in a vain attempt to restore the offending item but Staff said sharply, 'You'd better go and check it properly before you leave the ward.' She handed her a file. 'Dr Stevington wants Mr Warner to have another X-ray on that hip before he makes a final decision about operating so you'd better take him down now. You'll just about have time. I've telephoned to say you're coming and they know it's fairly urgent, so off you go. Oh, and Nurse, try not to lose him if at all possible.'

'Yes, Staff, I mean . . . no, Staff.'

The wheelchair was manoeuvred easily along the corridor and into the lift. X-ray was still busy and a third-year nurse greeted their arrival with an apologetic smile.

'I'm afraid you'll have to wait a few minutes, Mr Warner. The radiographer has a patient in with him now and there's another waiting, but it shouldn't take too long.'

'That's all right, love, it makes a change to get out of the ward for a bit. I'm quite happy sitting here.'

With a smile the girl hurried away to return minutes later. 'We can see to you now, Mr Warner.' She looked at Emma. 'It shouldn't take more than a couple of minutes. Can you hang on only we can't really spare anyone to bring him back to the ward.'

'That's all right, I can wait.'

'Fine, is this his file?'

Emma handed it over. 'Staff would like it back please and Dr Stevington will need to see the fresh X-rays tomorrow morning when he does his round.'

'I'll see what we can do.' The patient was wheeled away and Emma found herself wondering how she would enjoy her stint in this type of department when the time came. Quite a lot of nurses, she knew, looked forward to Casualty and Outpatients. They preferred what was a quick through-put of patients where one simply didn't have the time to become involved. Personally she liked the wards, where people became personalities rather than just a file and case notes, even if there were times when she had to battle with tears if one of them died or went home. Mike was right, there was a distinction between attention to the patients' needs and emotion, and as yet she still hadn't entirely learned to separate the two.

The door opened and a tap on her arm sent her whirling round to find herself looking up at Phil.

'For heaven's sake,' she hissed, gazing round in terror in case Sister was lurking in the near vicinity. 'What are you doing here?'

He grinned. 'I was just on my way to Cas. when I thought I recognised that mop of hair and it was too good an opportunity to miss.'

She found it hard to be annoyed when he looked at her like that. 'I've just brought a patient down to X-ray.'

'Well his X-ray is my good fortune then. I'd been hoping to see you. I just wanted to make sure you didn't get into trouble yesterday when the Great White Chief bumped into us. I'm sorry, I should have realised . . .'

'It wasn't your fault,' she protested, whilst thinking that that wasn't entirely true. 'Anyway, as it happens, no I didn't. How about you?'

'The air has been a shade cool but he hasn't actually said anything.' He saw her brown eyes widen anxiously and he brushed his lips against hers. 'For heaven's sake, don't worry about it.'

'Yes, but he is your boss. You have to work with him.'

'He has no complaint where my work is concerned and he knows it. Anyway, he's probably just sour because his own love life isn't going so well.'

His own love life. Emma frowned. 'I didn't realise he had a love life.' She wondered why it should come as such a shock.

'My dear girl,' Phil looked at her mockingly, 'he may be my boss but he's human like the rest of us.' He laughed softly. 'You really are naïve aren't you?'

A sudden, vivid memory of being encircled by the Senior Registrar's strong, muscular arms brought the colour rushing to her face. 'I just hadn't thought about it,' she muttered. Garrard Blair was just a figure in a white coat. Ice-cool and efficient, inhuman. Except that there had been nothing inhuman about that kiss. Taken aback, she wondered how she could possibly have imagined that there wouldn't be a girlfriend or even a wife in his life. 'Anyway, I'm really not interested,' she snapped crossly.

Phil laughed. 'Rumour has it that his girlfriend isn't either. She broke off their engagement, which must make things a little difficult and no doubt explains why he's like a bear with a sore head.'

'Why, what do you mean?' she asked, despising herself for being drawn.

'Only that she is Sir Geoffrey Halston's daughter,' he suggested, and saw her eyes widen.

'Not the consultant?'

'The very same. Practice in Harley Street and all that. Oh yes, our beloved Senior Registrar would have done very nicely for himself there, but apparently the delectable Jane found that all work and no play makes Garrard a very dull boy.'

Emma found herself vaguely resenting the sneering note in his voice. 'I would have thought, being a doctor's daughter herself, that she would have wanted to do everything she could to help his career.'

'Well there's no accounting for taste.' Phil smiled lazily down at her. 'Put your claws back, kitten, before I start getting the idea that you're smitten by the great man yourself.'

'Oh rubbish,' Emma snapped, and then, as she saw Sister's navy-clad figure looming in the distance, 'for heaven's sake go or we'll both be in trouble again.'

But to her dismay he made no move to do as she asked and Emma closed her eyes as Sister Fox bore down upon them, her face frosty with displeasure.

'Nurse, what are you doing standing around getting in everyone's way?' The sharp voice broke off and Emma watched, fascinated, as Sister's expression changed. 'Oh, Dr Carrington, I didn't realise . . .'

'That's all right, Sister,' Phil's voice was a gentle drawl. 'I just happened to be passing and as it's my tea break anyway,' he glanced at his watch, 'I thought I'd pop in . . .'

Sister Fox was really quite attractive when she

smiled. 'As it happens I was just about to have a cup myself, Doctor, and you're more than welcome to join me.' Her hand gestured him towards the office and she glanced impatiently at Emma. 'Nurse, your patient is waiting to be taken back to the ward, I suggest you get a move on.'

Beyond Sister's shoulder Emma caught Phil's broad wink. It took the edge off Sister's sharpness and she managed to stop herself smiling as she lowered her head and muttered submissively, 'Yes, Sister.'

All the same, as she wheeled Mr Warner and the file back into the lift, she couldn't help remembering rather crossly just how readily he had switched on the charm and managed to soothe Sister's ruffled feathers.

I'm being ridiculous, she told herself firmly, as the doors slid open and she headed for Men's Surgical. All he did was save us both from getting into trouble.

None of which served to erase a vague feeling of resentment.

CHAPTER EIGHT

SISTER Meredith's expression darkened as Nurse Beech slipped into the office adjusting the pink belt over her apron as she murmured an apology.

'Sorry, Sister, the bus was late.'

Laura Meredith's gaze rose, pointedly, to the clock on the wall of her office. 'Day staff begin duties on the ward at eight o'clock promptly, Nurse, which means that I expect you to be here at least five minutes earlier in order to take over from the night staff. Having worked all night I fail to see why they should be kept waiting because my staff get out of bed too late to catch a bus. I would suggest that in future either you acquire a more adequate alarm clock or catch an earlier bus. Do I make myself perfectly clear?'

'Yes, Sister. Sorry, Sister.'

The night report book lay open on the desk. 'Mr Thornton had a good night and didn't need a sedative. He seems to be getting over his operation well and is responding well to his medication. Who do we have next, Staff?'

'Mr Harris, Sister.'

'Ah yes, now he isn't feeling too well. Mr Blair will be seeing him this morning during rounds and will want to make a thorough examination, so be sure the necessary trolleys are ready.' She looked at the gathered group and leaned to one side. 'Nurse Benedict, did you sleep in that apron?'

Emma stared at her, then down at the apron. It did look slightly creased. 'No, Sister.'

'Well change it please before appearing on my ward.'

'Yes, Sister.' She sighed. It was going to be one of those days. She knew it the moment she heard the Senior Registrar's name mentioned.

'Mr Warner didn't have a very good night. Night Staff didn't wake him with tea this morning at seven so he is still sleeping now. Let him rest as long as he likes and see to it that he has something to eat if he wants it when he wakes.

'Yes, Sister.'

The routine of the Kardex went on. Each patient's progress was noted and instructions for the day's work given before they filed out on to the ward. It was eight-thirty. Most of the walking patients had already been awake for over an hour and had just finished breakfast. Those due for operations huddled beneath the blankets wishing the day was over.

Emma cleared plates and cups on to the trolley, wheeled it from the ward and began swabbing down lockers, handing out the morning post, chatting with patients and taking temperatures. It was a normal, hectic morning but somehow, as always, by the time the white-coated figure of the Senior Registrar appeared, the ward was running smoothly.

Emma congratulated herself on having escaped running into Garrard Blair as she walked beside the trolley escorting a drowsy patient to theatre. She felt just slightly guilty at having manoeuvred it, except that Mike hadn't minded when she had offered to take his place.

'I'm sure he'd much prefer to hold your hand than mine and I can't blame him. Anyway, I've still got to get the rest of the medicines out. As long as Sister doesn't mind.'

Sister didn't. On the contrary, she received the request with brisk approval. 'I'm delighted to see you taking an interest, Nurse, in fact I may say I have been pleased to see a distinct improvement in your attitude during the past week. I'm pleased to think our little chat served some useful purpose.'

If only she knew, Emma thought, quickening her steps as the porters wheeled the trolley along the corridor towards theatre and, smiling down at her patient, felt his grip tighten on her hand.

'You're going to be fine, Mr Patterson, and I shall be waiting for you as soon as you come back to the ward.' Her concern was genuine. She liked Albert Patterson who faced a serious abdominal operation and who had confessed to her, quietly, that he hoped he wouldn't recover consciousness. The admission had shocked her.

'There's nothing to go back to, you see,' he had said. 'Not since the wife died, and I feel I've outlived my usefulness now, so it would be better you see.'

Emma had tried to convince him that he had to fight but knew it was a losing battle and had gone into the sluice to shed a few angry tears that age and loneliness could make someone want to give up. Well, for the moment Albert Patterson was in the hands of the surgeons, men like Garrard Blair. Without consciously being aware of it Emma's steps quickened as she hurried back along the corridor to the ward.

The ward round should be over now with a bit of luck, the thought brought a smile to her face, giving it a gamine attractiveness of which she was totally unaware as she made her way into the ward and the frowning presence of Helen Blake who beckoned her perfunctorily and said in a low voice, 'Ah, there you are, Nurse, come and give me a hand with this new admission. He's just been brought up from Casualty.'

Emma bustled to one side of an empty bed, Staff to the other, and together they straightened the sheet, drawing back the covers. Two porters eased a young man on to the bed.

'There we are, Staff. He's all yours and you might find him a bit of a handful. He'd had a bit to drink before he finally wrapped his car round a tree.'

'Thanks, John. I expect we'll cope.' Helen Blake smiled pleasantly as she took the brief notes and the porters left the ward. 'Oh well, he looks peaceful enough now.' She frowned as she studied the young man. His face was pale, showing more clearly the ugly lacerations and a dark bruise which had already formed, swelling beneath one eye.

Emma felt herself shiver and wondered if she would ever get used to seeing some of the more horrific injuries which came in and be able to deal with them as calmly as Staff Nurse Blake.

'Barry Lawson, aged twenty-two,' Staff read through the notes quickly. 'Severe lacerations,' she bent to look more closely at the stitches. 'He's lucky, someone's done a good job on those. I doubt he'll have more than a very faint scar. Concussion, fractured tib and fib,' her fingers moved to the saline drip. 'Check his PTR, Nurse, and do it half-hourly until he has come round properly from the anaesthetic.'

'Yes, Staff.'

'And quietly please, Nurse.' Helen Blake looked at her watch. 'Mr Blair's round is running later than usual.'

Emma's hand, reaching for the thermometer, jerked and sent it spinning to the floor where it shattered into tiny fragments. She stared at it aghast, conscious of Staff's glacial expression.

'Clear it up, Nurse. Fetch a replacement and for heaven's sake get a move on.' She walked away on soft-soled shoes leaving Emma to brush up the offending pieces and retreat with them, hoping Sister wouldn't notice. Luckily the curtains remained firmly drawn round a bed at the end of the ward as she passed by, but she could hear the Senior Registrar's voice and automatically her steps quickened until she had reached the safety of the kitchen.

She stood for a few seconds recovering her breath. Really, it was ridiculous the effect that man had on her. The mere thought of that autocratic gaze turned in her direction was enough to turn her into a quivering mass.

She returned to the ward, sickeningly aware of the squeaks her shoes were making as she passed the bed again and instinctively she rose on to her tiptoes. She had just skirted the bed when the curtains swished back and Sister's voice brought her to a standstill.

'Nurse Benedict, what on earth do you think you are doing?'

Emma swallowed hard and turned. Her heart sank as another figure moved from behind the curtains. 'I . . . er, nothing, Sister.'

The Senior Registrar's gaze rose with a brief frown of annoyance from the case notes he was studying. The dark eyes narrowed as they passed over Emma then, to her relief, she was obviously dismissed from his thoughts as he said brusquely, 'I'm not too happy about Mr Thornton's progress, Sister. I think we'll try a different antibiotic and see if that does the trick. I don't suppose the results of the swabs are back yet?'

'No, sir, but I'll see what I can do to hurry them up.' Sister signalled to Nurse Beech who hurriedly rearranged the curtains and went to ensure that the patient was made comfortable again before she took the file and followed the Senior Registrar to the next bed.

'Nurse.'

Emma stiffened. 'Yes, Sister.'

'Make some coffee please and bring it along to my office. You have time, sir?'

He barely glanced at his watch. Emma had the feeling that his entire life was probably run like clockwork. 'Just about, Sister, if it doesn't take too long.'

'I'm sure it won't, sir.' Her glance in Emma's direction was full of meaning and Emma shuffled uncertainly.

'But I have to take Mr Lawson's temperature, Sister.'

'Nurse Richards will attend to it, Nurse.' The warning glance was sufficient. Emma headed for the kitchen, resentfully splashing milk into a sauce-

pan and banging it on to the stove. 'Coffee,' she
muttered. 'As if we hadn't better things to do.' She
slammed sugar on to the tray, set out two cups and
saucers and stood on tiptoe trying to reach the
coffee. Why were cupboards always so maddeningly beyond her reach?

She was straining up towards the shelf when a
hand reached out and a voice with a sharp note of
irritation in it said, 'For heaven's sake, here, let me,
before we have another accident on our hands.
Didn't anyone ever teach you to keep things where
they can be easily reached in safety?'

Pink-faced, Emma tugged furiously at her dress,
wondering miserably whether he had been standing
there long enough to have seen the vast expanse of
black-stockinged leg which she must have been
displaying. His face, however, was expressionless
beyond a slight quivering at the corners of his
mouth.

'Most people *can* reach,' she retorted crossly,
and wondered why, beside him, she felt even less
than her five feet two inches. She realised he wasn't
looking at her and out of the corner of her eye
followed his gaze. With a screech she leapt to
rescue the saucepan of rapidly rising milk and
began ladling generous spoonsful of coffee into
each cup. What was he doing sneaking up on her in
the kitchen anyway, she thought, and glowered at
him, defying him to say anything.

'We don't have any biscuits.' Her mouth compressed as she nearly added 'and you don't deserve
them anyway'. 'The coffee is almost ready.'

'That's all right.' He was leaning placidly against
the cupboard. 'Sister has been called away so

there's no point in cluttering her office. I'll have it here instead.'

Emma's eyes widened with horror. Senior Registrars didn't stand in the kitchen drinking their coffee. 'It's really no trouble, sir, and I'm sure Sister wouldn't mind.'

'I'm sure she won't,' he said, interpreting her thoughts with disconcerting accuracy, 'but I have drunk coffee in a kitchen before and I'm sure it won't hurt me to do so again.'

Emma stared at the tray and tried to imagine a man like Garrard Blair drinking coffee in a cosy little kitchen somewhere, probably first thing in the morning with his hair rumpled and needing a shave. She smiled at the image, then blinked hard as she realised he was watching her and frowning. Her heart missed a beat. Surely he couldn't have read her thoughts this time?

'Just how old are you, Nurse Benedict?' He spooned sugar generously into his cup.

Emma swallowed hard. 'Tw . . . twenty, sir.' The fact that she had celebrated her birthday a mere three weeks ago was not, she felt, any business of his.

'Really?' There was a vague note of mockery in the dark eyes as he looked at her. 'You look as if you should still be in the schoolroom. Certainly far too young to be a nurse.'

Her hand jerked spasmodically against the spare cup she had been about to remove from the tray and she watched, transfixed, as it rolled inexorably towards the edge of the cupboard and hit the floor, shattering into tiny pieces.

She bent to pick them up, fighting the tears that

suddenly filled her eyes. It wasn't fair. He had absolutely no right to imply that she wasn't old enough to be efficient at her job. She sniffed, then jumped as a hand closed over hers, taking the broken pieces of crockery from her frozen grasp.

'Just as well it's not the best china.'

Her heart seemed to perform a crazy little dance as their eyes met, then he straightened up, saying brusquely, 'Oh come on, it really isn't that bad. We'll dispose of these, then Sister will never know.' He tossed them into the bin and she watched, thinking that he could be far too nice when he wanted to be.

'I'm sorry.' She hoped he hadn't noticed the tear she dashed away quickly with her hand but, mercifully, he wasn't looking at her. He was putting away the coffee.

'My dear girl,' his voice was quite calm, 'accidents happen.' He frowned. 'Admittedly to some people more often than others. I didn't mean to imply that you weren't perfectly capable of doing your job. That *is* what you were thinking?'

'Well . . . I don't see that age has anything to do with it, and it's hardly my fault if I look younger than I am.'

'I agree.' His voice had suddenly hardened. 'But it is perhaps all the more reason why you should be wary about getting involved with experienced characters like Phil Carrington.'

Emma felt the colour rush from her cheeks. 'I . . . I don't know what you mean.'

'I think you know perfectly well what I mean.' His voice was very quiet and she found it hard to know whether he was angry or not. 'I do see what goes on around me and I also know young Carrington. He is not your type, Nurse Benedict.'

Emma stiffened with resentment. Just how did he know what was her type? She was on the point of telling him, pointedly, that it was really none of his business when she remembered just in time that nurses, and especially very junior nurses, didn't say such things to Senior Registrars.

'I fail to see how you can possibly know what my type is, sir, and in any case I assure you I'm perfectly capable of taking care of myself.' She wondered, crossly, why he should care what she did with her off-duty periods, then reminded herself that his concern was purely professional. Well he needn't worry. She wasn't likely to do anything that would reflect upon the good name of St Clement's.

'I doubt very much whether you know anything about a man like Carrington,' he said, the dark brows drawn together angrily. 'He'd eat a mouse like you for breakfast. In heaven's name, why him?'

She felt like saying 'Because he asked me,' but clamped her mouth into a rigid line instead. 'I really don't see . . .'

'No, you're right,' he snapped. 'It's none of my business. But if you go looking for trouble don't be surprised if you find it. But then, I dare say you'll cope. I obviously misjudged you, Nurse Benedict. And now, if you'll excuse me, I have to get back to theatre.'

He was gone, leaving her standing openmouthed and trembling. Just what did he mean by saying that he had misjudged her? Come to think of it, what right had Garrard Blair to judge her at all?

CHAPTER NINE

ALL thoughts of the Senior Registrar and his high-handed manner were pushed to one side, however, as the day developed into a hectic rush to get everything done.

Sister Meredith went off-duty at one o'clock, having handed over to Sister Travers whose reputation for iron discipline and the sharpness of her tongue kept everyone on their toes.

Bustling down the ward with a bag of soiled linen, Sue Harper flung a pointed look in the direction of the office and hissed, 'That's the third bed I've had to completely remake. As if we hadn't enough to do.'

Emma threw her a smile of sympathy and whispered a warning as the blue-clad figure emerged and advanced like a thundercloud in their direction. 'Look out! Here comes the dragon and she's breathing fire.'

Flinging a look of thanks over her shoulder Sue fled and Emma bent her head even lower over the chart on which she was entering the PTR readings of a patient only recently back from theatre, hoping fervently that nothing she had inadvertently done was the cause of the look of irritation on Sister Travers' face. Hope faded as the sharp voice reached her.

'Nurse Benedict, haven't you finished that job yet? There are other patients equally in need of your attention.'

Caroline Travers' glance swept the length of the ward with icy disapproval. 'Those castors are not in line, kindly see to it. And straighten the cover on Mr Thornton's bed.' Her tongue clicked her annoyance. 'Really, I sometimes wonder what you girls learn in PTS these days. Surely they taught you how to turn in the corners?'

Emma lowered her head in a gesture of meekness she was far from feeling. 'Yes, Sister.'

'Well I don't see much evidence of it.'

It was a pity, Emma thought, that someone as attractive as Sister Travers should have such an unfortunate manner. Unfortunate because it not only meant that the staff were constantly having to redo jobs which to anyone else would have seemed perfectly satisfactory, thus having less time to spend on more important things, but it also created an atmosphere which conveyed itself to the patients, leaving them edgy each time she walked on to the ward.

Looking at the dark, sleekly-coiled hair and the delicately made-up features, Emma wondered how much truth there was in the rumours that Sister Travers' marriage was undergoing a great deal of strain or had even broken down completely. If it was true, Emma thought, then she couldn't help but feel sorry for the young woman who, at just thirty, already seemed soured by life.

She looked at Sister's hand. There were no rings. Not that that meant much. Even though wedding rings were permitted there were some nurses who still preferred not to wear them on duty, or who wore them on a chain round their necks.

Even Helen Blake looked harassed as she followed the tall figure down the ward.

'The whole of the afternoon's list has had to be altered, Staff. Grace Ward have had two emergency admissions which means their patients have had to be put back, and we have one coming up in the next half-hour.' She looked at her watch. 'How many have we left still to go up to theatre?'

'Three, Sister. Mr Chattarhagee has already been given his pre-med.'

'Then he had better go now. I've spoken to Theatre Sister and we're to hold the others back until they give the go-ahead. Of course it makes things worse that Mr Hetherington had to cancel his list yesterday and they're trying to fit in as many as possible today.'

'I gather he had to attend his father-in-law's funeral, Sister.'

'So I believe.'

Standing patiently to one side, Emma gained the distinct impression that Sister Travers' only concern was for the efficient running of her ward, and that she resented any kind of disruption. She waited as Sister sat behind the desk studying the report book and Staff returned to the ward.

'I understand that young Paul Squires is to have another operation, possibly tomorrow.'

Emma's face clouded. 'Oh no.'

'I gather the prospects aren't too good but this is one of those situations where to do nothing would be more dangerous than to leave things to take their course.'

'Yes, Sister.'

'Well, Mr Whittaker is very good. He couldn't be

in better hands. Naturally he's going to need some specialling after the operation. I think it would be best if he went into one of the side-rooms when he comes back to us, Nurse. See to it that everything is ready.'

'Yes, Sister, I'll get on to it straight away.'

'By the way, you may as well know now, Sister Meredith is leaving.'

Emma's eyes widened. 'Oh no. I'm sorry, Sister. She'll be missed.'

'Yes.' There was a hint of defensiveness in Sister Travers' voice. 'I'm sure she will. St Clement's will miss her too. She's almost become part of the establishment!' A smile briefly touched Caroline Travers' lips, giving a momentary illusion of prettiness.

'But surely she doesn't need to retire yet,' Emma said. 'I thought she had quite a few more years to go.'

'I doubt if many people know her real age. In fact she could stay on for another eighteen months, but she has asked for early retirement on the grounds of ill health—though that isn't general knowledge and I'm sure she wouldn't want it to be circulated.'

'No, of course not, Sister. Do you know what the problem is?'

Sister's shoulders rose. 'I gather her heart is not as strong as it should be.'

'Oh no.'

'The doctors have advised her to take things easy and she is sensible enough to take that advice. I rather think she intends sharing a little cottage in the country with her sister, a widow.'

'That sounds like a good idea, Sister.'

'Yes, I'm sure it is. The point is, I think we should start some sort of collection and begin making discreet enquiries as to what sort of gift would be most acceptable. I'm sure everyone will want to donate. Doctors and senior staff will make their own collection, of course, but I thought you might speak to the nurses and between us we should be able to get something particularly nice.'

'I'd be happy to start it off, Sister. It should be easy enough to do it without her knowing anything about it.'

'I'd be most grateful if you will. Perhaps when we know the sort of sums involved we can have a quiet meeting between the staff to discuss it. I've already had a very generous donation from Mr Blair.'

'You mean he knows, Sister?'

'Yes, he does. I believe it was he who confirmed the heart condition, though she must have suspected for some time before she went to talk to him.'

Poor Sister Meredith, Emma thought, remembering only too clearly now the number of occasions when she had seen the look of weariness on the older woman's face and had merely put it down to the busy routine which was always a part of Men's Surgical.

'Actually, she is taking it rather well,' Sister Travers was saying. 'And the last thing she would want is for people to start making a fuss, so as far as everyone else is concerned, apart from the staff on this ward and the few other people who already know the truth, she is simply leaving because she has decided to take an early retirement and make

way for someone younger. In any case she won't be
leaving us for some months yet.'

There was something in Sister's expression which
made Emma wonder suddenly whether this meant
that Sister Travers was hoping to become a perma-
nent feature on Men's Surgical herself. If so she
wasn't at all sure that she was going to enjoy her
remaining time on the ward. She kept her thoughts
to herself, however, as she accepted her dismissal
and made her way back to the ward to begin getting
the side-room ready. It was strange how she had
often thought of Laura Meredith as an adversary
and yet now that the possibility of her going had
arisen, she was suddenly aware that she would
miss her in spite of her insistence upon what some
might think of as the old-fashioned kind of discipline.

Emma sighed. There was nothing old-fashioned
about Sister Travers. She was simply one of those
nurses who, whilst undeniably efficient and good at
her job, seemed to lack the kind of compassion and
patience which would have made her an outstand-
ing nurse.

She flicked the crisp, clean sheets over the bed,
neatly tucking in the corners as she had been taught
in PTS. In the distance the telephone rang and
minutes later Staff walked into the room.

'Mr Sinclair is going up to theatre today after all,
Nurse, so we should be getting him back possibly
tonight or tomorrow, depending on how he comes
through it. Check the oxygen supply will you, and
remove one of those pillows. That's right.'

Staff bustled out again and Emma continued
automatically with her work. The routine went on,

just as it would even if she were to cease being part
of it. There was something vaguely depressing
about the thought.

CHAPTER TEN

IT WAS several days since Emma had last seen Phil, and then only from a distance. First there had been her own off-duty, then he had apparently had a long weekend. She thought she had seen his red sports car roaring out through the hospital gates and had felt a slight twinge of disappointment that he hadn't taken the trouble to say goodbye or at least to mention that he was going. Not that there was any reason why he should, of course, she told herself, as she set up a trolley for a blanket bath. All the same, the feeling lingered. After that she had caught only a fleeting glimpse of him as he was going into Casualty, but he had been in a hurry, which was probably why he hadn't seen her when she waved, even though he had been looking in her direction.

He probably had a lot on his mind, she told herself. Especially if Garrard Blair was keeping him on his toes, which probably explained why he hadn't even been able to see her long enough to let her know what time he would be picking her up that evening for the dance. If I ever manage to get finished in time myself, she thought, as she loaded a jug of hot water on to the trolley, checked the waterproof mackintosh and other items then paused as another thought occurred.

'Perhaps he's forgotten he asked me,' she said aloud.

Sue glanced over her shoulder, warily checking on Sister's whereabouts. 'Rubbish. Why on earth should he have forgotten?'

'Oh I don't know. No reason at all.' Emma forced a lightness into her voice. 'I expect I'm just getting the jitters. I spent half my pay packet on a new dress and I'd hate to see it all go to waste.'

'Well I don't see why it should. You're worrying for nothing.'

Emma hoped she was right, though she couldn't entirely banish the thought that there had been another figure, a female figure, in the passenger seat of the red sports car. Not that he wasn't perfectly entitled to invite whoever he liked to ride in his own car.

'It's not a very sexy dress,' she said. She donned her waterproof apron.

'Well for heaven's sake, you're not the sexy type.'

'Oh thanks.' She looked abashed and Sue retracted hastily.

'Oh come on, you know what I mean. I just meant that skin-tight trousers look fine on some people, but not on you.' She stood with her hands on her hips. What are you wearing anyway?'

Emma giggled. 'Not skin-tight trousers anyway. Actually, it's just a plain little dress, though it didn't seem like it somehow when I tried it on. In fact it looked rather nice—only now I'm not so sure.'

'You'll feel different when you've got your make-up on and done your hair.' Sue studied the trolley reflectively. 'Do you suppose we really do all look the same in uniform?'

Emma's eyes widened in horror. 'Oh lord, I hope not, otherwise he may not recognise me at all.'

'I shouldn't think there's much danger of that, not with that hair.'

'Don't,' she wailed. 'Red hair can be a distinct disadvantage.' It means you can't hide, she thought, and felt her pulses flame as the darkly handsome features of Garrard Blair swam for no reason at all into her mind. 'Come on, we'd better get cracking before Sister tracks us down.'

She wheeled the trolley into the ward and for the next hour was kept busily occupied in blanket bathing those patients who were too ill to be moved or who weren't allowed out of bed. It was a job she had dreaded when she first came out of PTS. It was one thing to practise on a dummy but the reality of bathing a patient was quite different. She had quickly learned, however, that the job could be done quickly and efficiently and without any loss of dignity to the patient, and that the feeling of being clean and refreshed meant a lot to patients who were very ill.

'There we are, Mr Miller, isn't that better?'

The elderly patient smiled up at her, his eyes heavy with tiredness. 'Thank you, Nurse, much better.'

'I'll just give your shoulders and back a light dusting of powder then we can slip your pyjama jacket back on and you can go to sleep again.' She helped him to sit up and refastened the buttons for him when his own fingers fumbled. 'Are you expecting any visitors today?' she chattered as she re-loaded the trolley and tidied the bed covers.

'I think my daughter and her family are coming, if the weather isn't too bad. It's quite a bus ride for them. I told her not to bother but she says she wants to come.'

'Well I'm sure she does. Anyway it's stopped raining and it'll cheer you up to have someone to talk to. Is there anything I can get you? How about a book? The WVS ladies will be round with the trolley later this afternoon you know.' She left him contentedly propped up against his pillows looking pink and shiny and reading his newspaper while she hurried back to empty the trolley before starting on the pile of soiled linen that had to be sorted.

It was a busy morning and she was glad when Sister finally sent her off to lunch. She met Sally on the stairs and they went into the cafeteria together, groaning as they viewed the inevitable crowd. But they managed to find a table and carried their loaded trays towards it. Sally sat down with a groan, pushing her shoes off and wriggling her toes with sighs of relief.

'I'm never going to get through the rest of the day. My feet are killing me already. As for the dance tonight, I must be mad.'

Emma studied her food cautiously and prodded an object lying submerged in a layer of custard. 'Is that a plum? I hate plums. I thought it was apple pie.'

Sally leaned forward. 'It's a plum. Here, swop it for my treacle pudding. My appetite has suddenly vanished anyway and I'll never get into my dress if I eat all this.'

Emma tucked into her shepherd's pie with the uninhibited enthusiasm of one who doesn't have to worry about her weight. Her plate empty, she pushed it aside and spooned sugar into her coffee, listening idly to the amazing crescendo of noise as so many people gathered together.

'I just hope we're not late getting off tonight,' Sally said. 'If I don't shampoo my hair it won't be fit to be seen.'

Emma thought it looked very nice. It always did. Not like her own, she thought miserably. She drained her cup and stood up. 'How about some more coffee? The queue's gone down a bit. I'll get some.'

She eased her way through the crowd, stepping aside to let someone pass with a loaded tray when a pair of hands suddenly closed round her waist. She was blushing even before she turned round.

'Hi, I've been looking for you. Have you been deliberately avoiding me, Nurse Benedict, my angel?' Phil planted a kiss on her cheek.

She thought he might have chosen a slightly less public place, as a group of medical students who were obviously with Phil made varying comments and noises of appreciation. But she forgave him as he gave an unrepentant grin.

'No, of course I haven't been avoiding you,' she said. 'I've just been busy, that's all.'

'Excuses, excuses. I was beginning to think you were trying to back out of our date.'

He couldn't be serious, she thought, trying desperately not to remember the image of a girl beside him in the red sports car, or to let her gaze wander to where Amanda Collins was sitting in a far corner of the cafeteria looking red-eyed and unattractively miserable. So things obviously hadn't worked out. Or perhaps she hadn't been the girl in question. She wondered, with a vague spasm of pity for the girl, whether Phil even cared.

'I'll pick you up about eight, then?'

'What?' She jerked back to the realisation that he was speaking. 'Oh, yes, fine.' She tried not to see one of the medical students winking broadly at her. She pretended she hadn't seen him as she lowered her head and marched stiffly to the serving counter to join the queue.

Returning to the table she put the dishes down.

'Soup?' Sally stared at it. 'You can't still be hungry. I thought you went for coffee.'

Emma gazed at the thick cream of mushroom and felt her stomach tighten. She hadn't even noticed what she had picked up. She lifted her spoon defensively and took a mouthful. 'Well, we might not have time to eat again before we go out tonight.'

She spent the afternoon feeling sick. And if I never see a dish of mushroom soup again it will be too soon, she thought, wishing she could just curl up in bed and sleep it off. Unfortunately Sister had other ideas.

'Nurse Benedict,' she strode down the ward just as Emma let in the first of the afternoon's visitors. 'I hear you enjoy cooking.'

Emma blinked. It was true. Whenever she went home for the weekend she enjoyed spending an afternoon in her mother's kitchen helping to make bread or rich fruit cakes. But how did Sister know that?

'Yes, Sister.'

'Good. Into the kitchen then and start helping

Nurse Beech to butter bread for the patients' tea. The kitchen staff are having problems again, with so many off sick. Come along now, get a move on, and when you've finished report to Staff Nurse Blake and help with the medicines.'

'Yes, Sister.'

For the next hour she buttered slices of bread, ladled jam into dishes, sliced fruit cake and dispensed them from the trolley with cups of tea.

Emma paused at the foot of Mr Patterson's bed. The old man hadn't any visitors and was lying huddled beneath the blankets with his eyes closed. She felt a stab of concern because, even though he had come through his operation well and mercifully nothing awful had been found, he didn't seem to be making as much progress as was expected.

Going closer she said softly, 'I've brought you a cup of tea Mr Patterson. Do you think you could manage one?' For a moment she thought perhaps he was asleep until he opened his eyes to stare at her. She was horrified to see a solitary tear roll down his leathery cheek.

'I'm sorry, Nurse.'

She put the cup on the bedside locker and took his hand. 'Mr Patterson, what is it? What's wrong? Aren't you feeling well? Do you have a pain?' Her gaze anxiously scanned the ward for some sign of Sister or Staff, but neither were in evidence.

He brushed the tear away self-consciously. 'Just feeling sorry for myself I expect.'

'But you're doing very well. The operation was a success.'

'I know, and I should be grateful. I am grateful.' He blew his nose hard. 'But you see, it means I'm still here and I still have to face the loneliness, and I don't know that I can.' He broke off. 'I'm sorry. I didn't mean to complain. I know how busy you are.'

She shook her head. 'We're here to listen, to see if we can help. Have you any relatives at all? Any family?'

'None I'd want to go to if that's what you mean. I've no intention of becoming a burden.'

'Oh, but I'm sure they wouldn't look at it like that.'

'It's what I would feel.'

She bit her lip, recognising the kind of independence she saw in so many elderly patients who might be frail and old but who were determined to continue to live their own lives in their own homes even as they became physically less able to do so.

It was a growing problem, something they had discussed at length in PTS. Emma was genuinely concerned. 'Have you talked to anyone about how you feel?'

'Why should anyone be interested in my problems?'

'But of course they are. We all are, and I'm sure something can be sorted out.' She bit her lip, not quite sure what. 'Look, have a nice cup of tea while it's hot, and a piece of cake. It will cheer you up a bit, and try not to worry.'

She left him propped up against the pillows and waylaid Helen Blake. 'Oh, Staff, I'm a bit worried about Mr Patterson. I wonder if someone might have a chat with him.'

'In what way worried, Nurse?' She reached automatically for the Kardex. 'He seems to be getting over his operation very well. Progress is quite normal.'

'Oh yes, it's not that, Staff. It's just that he seems very depressed and I think it's because he's worried about going back home and coping on his own. He's very independent, but I think he feels lost since his wife died.'

'I see.' Staff scanned the Kardex. 'I see he has a son in Manchester.'

'Yes, I did ask him about relatives but he says he doesn't want to be a burden.'

'Mm. It happens quite often. Perhaps I'll have a word with him and get someone from Social Services to see what they can come up with. At least there are alternatives these days—sheltered accommodation for instance, where elderly people can live in flats, quite independently, but where they have the security of knowing that there is always a warden on the premises. Or possibly even a home-help may be the solution. Thank you for letting me know anyway, Nurse, I'll see to it and have a chat with Mr Patterson and try to put his mind at rest.'

'Oh thank you, Staff.'

'You'd better start clearing the tea things, Nurse, and then you can see to the flowers. By the way, well done. It's important to remember that helping to solve patients' personal problems matters every bit as much as curing their physical ills.'

'Yes, Staff.' Feeling suddenly ten feet tall Emma turned and hurried back to her work and for the rest of the afternoon even Sister seemed to be in a better mood.

CHAPTER ELEVEN

SHE rushed over to the Nurses' Home as soon as Staff told her she could go, and spent half an hour wallowing in a bath and washing her hair. Just as she padded along the corridor, swathed in a dressing gown and carrying her sponge bag, Sue rushed in, breathless and flushed.

'Oh lord, I'm never going to make it. I thought Sister was never going to let me go and she knows it's the dance tonight. I'll swear she was being awkward on purpose.' She was already unfastening her belt, flinging it on to the bed as she let herself into her room.

Emma followed, standing in the doorway. 'I've finished with the bathroom. Perhaps you'd better bag it before someone else does.'

'Thanks, I will.' Sue grabbed a towel. 'I'm starving. I wonder if I've got time for beans on toast.'

'Oh don't. So am I but if I stop to eat now I'll never get ready in time. It's going to take ages to do anything with my hair. I just hope there's a decent buffet tonight.'

'I should think there will be, especially as most of the bigwigs are likely to turn up. It's just about the one occasion in the year when everyone gets together and you don't have to stand on formality. Imagine,' Sue's eyes gleamed mischievously, 'all those doctors and dishy registrars.'

Emma's heart gave an odd little lurch. 'I

wouldn't have thought it would be their cup of tea.'

'Oh you'd be surprised.' Sue stepped out of her uniform. 'Can you imagine years ago, when it was more or less compulsory. You know, a bit like those awful dances Matron used to hold when she presided like royalty.'

'It sounds awful.'

'Well thank heavens things have changed, and I intend making the most of it. Get them when their defences are down I say. Of course you're all right. Lucky you. If you really like the Phil Carrington type.'

She glanced anxiously at her friend and Emma forced her lips into a smile, muttering something before she fled back to her own room where she sat in front of the mirror and closed her eyes, trying to imagine herself dancing in Phil's arms. The only trouble was, it wasn't Phil she saw. Maddeningly, it was Garrard Blair, looking devastatingly handsome and frowning down at her.

'Probably afraid I'll crush his toes as well as his fingers,' she muttered, and came back to reality with a bump. Not that he was likely to be there anyway, or would he? She drew herself up, tightening her stomach muscles, then let them sag again. For some reason she suddenly wished she wasn't going either, but it was too late to back out now even if she really wanted to—which she didn't, she told herself firmly. She'd have to be crazy even to think about it when every other female at St Clement's was falling over herself to go out with Phil Carrington.

She was prowling round her room, desperately trying to ignore the rumblings of her stomach and telling herself that she would not look out to see if there was any sign of his car, when he arrived, ten minutes late.

At least half a dozen times she had rushed into the bedroom to check her appearance in the long mirror and wondered whether the dress, with its swirling skirts and deeply frilled off the shoulder neckline, had really been a wise choice. It certainly made her look different. She had washed her hair and borrowed Sue's heated rollers, setting it into a much softer style than usual, and with a careful application of make-up, softly emphasising her eyes, the effect was quite startling. So much so that she had almost had second thoughts.

'Don't be ridiculous.' Sue had squashed them in her usual, forthright manner and given her whole-hearted approval as Emma pirouetted slowly, on delicately high-heeled shoes before her. 'You look gorgeous. I think our Dr Carrington is in for quite a surprise. Just remember before he sweeps you off your feet that he has the reputation of a starving wolf.'

'I'm not likely to forget,' Emma had laughed. 'As far as I'm concerned tonight is just for fun. I intend to enjoy myself and have a thoroughly marvellous time. But that's all.' She flicked back her hair and fixed her earrings. 'There, now what's the time. Oh lovely, just time for a coffee before he comes. Do you want one?'

'No thanks.' Sue scuttled for the door. 'I've still got to put my face on. I'll see you at the do.' She disappeared and Emma decided she would forego the coffee too. Her stomach was fluttering far too much to be able to eat or drink anything.

Phil came into the room while she collected her bag and the short fur jacket which had been a present from her parents last Christmas, and she couldn't help blushing when he gave a low, soft whistle of approval as he took her in his arms.

She knew she was probably being perverse, but she couldn't help feeling just the slightest sense of resentment at the look of surprise in his eyes as he came slowly towards her. She wondered what he had expected and then stopped wondering as he kissed her full on the mouth.

'Well, well, you've certainly done me proud.' He nibbled at her ear, sending shivers down her spine. 'You're quite a little butterfly.'

'You'd better watch out then,' she quipped, wondering why she felt so ridiculously nervous. 'I should warn you I turn back into a caterpillar at midnight.'

His lips twitched and she felt crazily elated that her words of wit hadn't gone unnoticed. 'This isn't quite the image of Nurse Benedict one gets on the ward.'

'But I'm not on the ward now,' she murmured, dropping her voice to what she hoped was a suitably sexy pitch.

'And I'm not complaining.' He brushed her hair aside so that he could nibble her ear again. 'It's funny, it's hard to tell you apart when you're in uniform, but I'm all in favour of surprises.'

She thought, fleetingly, that he didn't seem to have too much trouble recognising different nurses, or perhaps he wasn't worried who he flirted with.

'Are there any more in store?'

She blinked and was suddenly aware of his hand moving over the fabric of her dress, tracing the firmness of her breast. She detached herself with a nervous little laugh. 'Hadn't we better get going unless we're going to be late?'

'There's no hurry. Who wants to arrive first anyway?' He released her and smiled as he looked round the small room. 'We've got plenty of time for a drink first. Why don't we sit down and get cosy?' He patted the sofa cushion beside him and she laughed, breathlessly.

'Sorry, I don't have anything. I'm afraid we're not really allowed to bring drink into the Nurses' Home but I expect there will be plenty when we get to the dance.' She hovered hopefully near the door and saw the warmth rush out of his smile like an ice cube held under the hot tap.

He got to his feet, looking less than happy. 'Oh well, if prohibition is the rule I suppose we had better get going then before I, at least, die of thirst.'

She bit her lip, feeling ridiculous close to tears. 'I could easily have walked up to the main hall you know.' She half expected him to say that she could do that anyway but the faint look of boredom vanished.

'My dear girl, why do that when my chariot awaits at your door? In any case,' the smile was back again, 'I might not have stood a chance if you'd walked in alone looking like this.'

He seemed not to have noticed the jacket she was holding, so she shrugged herself quickly into it.

'Well I'm glad you approve.'

There was something nice about the proprietorial feel of his hand on her arm as they walked from the car, minutes later, up the slope and into the main hall where the dance was being held. It was going to be a nice evening, she told herself firmly. She was just getting all uptight about nothing and the best thing was just to relax and enjoy herself.

'I'll see you in a minute.' Suppressing a shiver of excitement, she left him and took her jacket along to the cloakroom, taking just long enough to check her hair and make-up before returning to where she had left him.

For a minute her heart missed a beat. He wasn't there. She stood, gazing around, hopping to one side as other couples came through the door, letting in a waft of freezing cold air. There was no sign of him. She wandered into the hall where a coloured spotlight was tracing patterns across the floor. It was already fairly crowded and her eyes searched the half-light for several seconds before she saw him leaning nonchalantly against the bar, surrounded by a group of friends. They were all making rapid headway into their drinks. Phil's pint was already reduced by half and she felt slightly injured that he hadn't waited for her, then told herself she was being unfair. After all, someone had probably launched one into his hand the minute he had walked into the hall.

She approached with a smile fixed on her face, trying not to feel like an insect under a microscope as several pairs of female eyes turned in her direction. They were all stunningly attractive, sipping at their cocktails, and suddenly she knew that her little cotton dress was all wrong. Why on earth hadn't Phil told her? Perhaps he hadn't known, or didn't care.

Perhaps he was blinded by her beauty, or was it just the brilliant spotlight that caused him to wince slightly as he turned in her direction and looked at her as if he was having trouble trying to remember who she was.

'Oh, there you are,' he said ungraciously.

She took the glass of sherry he held out to her, her teeth clashing against the glass as her mouth froze in an embarrassed smile. She sipped it politely, trying not to grimace. He might at least have asked her what she wanted instead of assuming. She had hated sherry ever since it had made her violently sick at a party a few Christmases ago. She hoped she wasn't going to be sick tonight. The thought brought her out in a cold sweat.

'What a pretty frock.'

One of the females, a slinky blonde who surely couldn't be a nurse, not with that figure and those looks, was draped like clinging ivy over her partner, her dress equally clinging, and exposing a shapely leg from beneath the slit skirt, glanced between inch-long eyelashes in Emma's direction and smiled.

Much, Emma supposed, as a cat might smile as it dragged in some dead and highly suspicious quarry. Christian Dior perfume wafted across as the female moved her mouth languidly from her glass to her boyfriend's neck. Perhaps she prefers blood, Emma thought, and suppressed a hysterical giggle by choking into her own glass.

Phil looked at her as if she was a lunatic. And he's probably right, she thought crossly. I shouldn't have come. I'm getting eaten alive and I haven't said a word yet. Why didn't he make it easier for her?

'Is that all right? I thought I'd get them in before the crush starts. Another half-hour and we won't be able to move in here.' His arm went round her waist and she smiled up at him, her mouth pouted for the kiss which was bound to come. It didn't and she licked her lips as if appreciating the sherry.

'Mm, yes, lovely.' It was just as well it was dark. Perhaps if they moved she could find a convenient plant pot somewhere and dispose of the contents of her glass before her stomach did. 'Actually I don't really drink . . .'

'How very boring for you,' Cat's-eyes murmured sweetly.

Phil looked momentarily peeved for some reason, then the smile flashed again. 'Well we'll soon change that, won't we, darling.' He nibbled at her ear. Perhaps he hadn't eaten either. Or perhaps the perfume, which had been a gift from Aunt Gloria, had been a mistake after all. Night of Passion wasn't exactly subtle, but it was all she had, and God knows she had been pretty sparing with it. 'Mm, very interesting. I don't know that one,' Phil frowned.

'Yes, it cost the earth,' she lied valiantly, and spilt sherry down the front of her dress as Phil's hand jerked suddenly under her arm.

'Of course you know Carol, don't you, my sweet?'

How could she possibly know anyone like that

and still be alive to tell the tale? 'No, I don't think . . .'

'Oh we've probably come across each other in Casualty,' the image said. 'I'm sure I've seen you scuttling in and out when I've been on duty.'

Feeling as if she was suddenly treading thirty feet of water without being able to swim, Emma twisted her sherry glass until its contents spun. 'Yes, that's probably it.' My God, she *is* a nurse. Carol . . . Carol. If only she could force her mouth to stop grinning.

'Of course I was on Women's Med before I got my Staff grading and moved to Casualty.'

That was it. Staff Nurse Peach. How could she have been so dense? It was the uniform, or lack of it, that made all the difference.

'I gather you're on Men's Surgical. Lucky you. All those gorgeous men.'

'Well, actually most of them are quite elderly and very ill, so they don't . . . I mean . . . well it's not . . .'

'Oh dear, the poor girl's blushing.'

Not only blushing but bursting into flames. She turned desperately to Phil who seemed to be sharing the laughter at her expense. Her glass clattered on to the bar. She wished she had never come. If she left now she could still have an early night. Her eyes filled with tears as she looked despairingly for the door, then Phil's hand was on her arm, guiding her away from his friends, but she could still hear their laughter ringing in her ears.

'Why don't we dance? Come on, I'm quite good at this particular little number.'

Without even waiting for her to speak she found

herself whirled on to the crowded floor and her head cradled against his chest. In fact her entire body felt as if it had been permanently welded to his as he held her, weaving her in and out of the other couples and every now and again raising her face to kiss her on the mouth.

The lump in her throat gradually lessened but she hated his friends. How could he be so marvellous and yet have such bad judgment, she wondered.

'Come on, cheer up. They were only teasing. They're always like that and you do invite it rather, you know.'

She blinked and he laughed. 'You look so ridiculously young and naïve. I've really never met anyone quite like you before. It's a novel experience and one I'm beginning to enjoy.'

Only beginning, she wondered. Well anyway, he probably couldn't pick and choose his friends so easily. After all, he had to work with those people.

She sighed and snuggled closer, shivering as his hands moved suggestively up and down her spine, not even caring who would see.

The music changed to something modern and they moved apart, gyrating with the rest of the couples, getting hotter and hotter as the air-conditioning seemed to have given up. She whirled and teetered on her high heels and fell, giggling, into Phil's arms, happy to stay there, breathing hard and not only from the exertion of the dance.

'It's getting crowded.'

'There's always a good turn out. Event of the year. Well judge for yourself.' Phil had to shout into her ear to make himself heard. 'Even the Great

White Chief has turned up. Not that he looks as if he's exactly enjoying himself does he?'

She twisted round and the smile faded on her lips as she saw Garrard Blair at the far side of the hall, looking incredibly tall and handsome in the dark evening suit. For some crazy reason her heart missed a beat. Somehow she hadn't expected that he would really turn up and he looked so different. For a moment, almost as if he became aware of her, he looked in her direction but gave no sign of recognition. Well after all, why should he, she thought, dully, and murmured, 'I'd hardly have thought this was his scene.'

'Oh I shouldn't think it is, but then, "England expects" and all that. It's the done thing. Puts everyone on the same level. Seniors fraternise with the lesser mortals.'

'How ridiculous,' Emma snapped with rare cynicism and saw Phil glance at her.

'So it is, but it still happens. Anyway I'm not exactly surprised the old man's looking sour. Look who he's talking to, and not getting the kind of response he'd like either, from the look of things.'

She had been trying not to look, but now her gaze was rivetted on the woman at Garrard Blair's side. She was tall, slim and elegant, her hair a short, neat cap of blonde curls, her dress an exquisite and obviously expensive confection of dateless silk chiffon.

'Who is she?' she heard herself ask through gritted teeth.

'Old Halston's daughter.'

'You don't mean . . . ?'

'The very same.'

No wonder he looked so grim.

'Probably trying to win her round again and she isn't having any, which must be a blow. Yes, he'd have done very nicely for himself with that little number as his wife and with Sir's name and reputation to back it all up.'

She felt a tiny flicker of anger well up inside her. 'Aren't you being a bit cynical? That sort of thing surely doesn't matter these days.'

'My dear girl, of course it does. A man in Blair's position could go a long way.'

'I should think a man like that could go equally as far on his own merit.'

'Ah yes, but it will be a whole lot easier with someone pulling a few strings along the way.'

She felt her colour rise. 'I suppose it doesn't occur to you that he may just love her. She's very beautiful.' Her voice sounded weak and grudging.

'And rich.' He laughed. 'Still, you could be right. He probably does have strictly honourable intentions. His sort usually do. Unfortunately it doesn't look as if the lady is prepared to play along, but then he has the night to work at it, and it's not really our problem is it, my sweet. Come on, let's dance.'

As he swung her into the rhythm, Emma contrived to keep glancing in the direction of the far side of the hall where the couple were deeply engaged in conversation, apparently oblivious to the noise and everything that was going on around them.

She wondered what they were saying, then shut them purposefully out of her mind. She twirled, her skirts billowing, as Phil danced with the kind of easy expertise which even seemed to make her own efforts look good. It was fun. Nice to forget Sister's eagle eye just for tonight, and she laughed as Phil caught her to him. Just as his mouth descended, she caught a glimpse over his shoulder of Garrard Blair's coldly disapproving stare.

He's got a nerve, she thought. I'm not on duty now. As if driven by some demon she purposefully draped her arm around Phil's neck and gazed dreamily into his eyes, murmuring in what she hoped was a sexy voice, 'Mm, this is lovely. I wish it could go on for ever.'

Surprise flickered momentarily in Phil's eyes, then turned to pleasure and something else she didn't quite want to read, before he clasped both his hands behind her back and pulled her close.

'It may not go on for ever my sweet, but we'll make the most of it while it does, won't we?'

She giggled nervously. She should have ditched that sherry but there hadn't been a chance. Phil had grabbed her arm, ordered her to drink up and the next thing she knew she had been in the middle of the dance floor. Of course it had only been one sherry, but a large one, and she hadn't eaten, which probably accounted for the fact that her knees felt so strange.

Still, dances were to enjoy and she wasn't going to let the Senior Registrar spoil it. When she looked in his direction again, however, disentangling herself from Phil's arms, he wasn't there and for some reason she felt cheated.

The music got steadily louder as the evening progressed and the hall got increasingly hotter. Excusing herself for a minute, Emma slipped out to the cloakroom and plunged her hands into cold water, pressing them against her flushed face. She looked a mess. Her lipstick had vanished, her nose was shiny and her feet ached. She had just eased off her shoe and was rubbing at her toes when Carol walked in, still looking fresh, make-up still intact and not a hair out of place—in spite of the fact that she had spent most of the evening draped around her boyfriend.

It's sickening, Emma thought, as she rammed her foot back into her shoe, wincing as it rubbed against the blister on her heel.

'Hi, I thought I saw you sneak out. Great evening, isn't it?'

'Great, super.'

'The band's very good. Better than last year.' Carol stared at her reflection, making a sultry pout as she applied another layer of lip gloss. 'But of course I don't suppose you were here for that.'

'No.' Emma chewed at her own lips to give them a little more colour. Why on earth had she rushed out leaving her evening bag on the table?

'Well, you're doing well. A good band *and* Phil.' Blue eyes studied her carefully for a moment before the mascara brush demanded their attention. 'I must say you're not his usual type, or at least you don't seem it, but then looks can be deceptive.' She gave a low laugh as she swung round, dropping the make-up back into her purse and snapping it to a close. 'Oh well, back into the fray, and the best of luck for the rest of the evening, but I'm sure you're going to have a whale of a time—Phil's the expert. I don't suppose we'll see you when you leave.' She winked broadly and wafted out, leaving Emma leaning faintly over a wash-basin wishing she could be sick.

She wasn't. Just deathly pale, but Phil didn't seem to notice as she put on a smile and slid back into place at his side. With a cursory glance in her direction he put another glass into her hand—a gin this time, a very large gin—before he carried on discussing the hospital rugger team with the six-foot giants who were presumably members of it. They, as the evening progressed, had got steadily noisier and redder about the face, Phil too, she noticed now, as she sipped at the drink and felt it lap like a tidal wave against the sherry already in her stomach.

For the next quarter of an hour she stood, shifting from one foot to the other, feeling as if he had forgotten her presence entirely. It was almost a relief in a way. It gave her time to look round. There was no sign of Garrard Blair. He had probably disappeared, as had a lot of the other couples, to the buffet which was now being served. Her stomach rattled and she tugged at Phil's arm.

'Just a minute, sweetie,' he said sharply.

'But I'm hungry and everyone else is going in.'

'Well for heaven's sake, if you can't wait go in by yourself and grab a plateful for me.'

Tears sprang to her eyes but she bit them back. She didn't fancy going in on her own but if she didn't eat something soon to mop up the drink she would pass out.

People began to drift back from the buffet in small laughing groups. There'll be nothing left, she thought, smiling grimly as she tried to ignore the gnawing pangs of emptiness. In fact she was just about past being hungry. The gin had helped to fill a space, and a tomato juice which she had bought for herself, unnoticed by Phil. No, she wasn't hungry after all. She burped.

'Must be getting my second wind.' She giggled at her own joke and felt Phil's quelling glance as he turned to look at her.

'Oh are you still here?'

Where else did he imagine she would be? If I had any spunk at all, she told herself firmly, I'd be anywhere but here. And she suddenly realised that, far from enjoying the evening, she felt thoroughly miserable. Most of it he had spent ignoring her, her feet were killing her and her head was spinning.

'I'd like to go,' she said.

'Go? Now?'

'Yes please.'

His mouth tightened as he glowered at his watch. 'Hell, it's only eleven o'clock. The evening's hardly started. Look, I think you're being a bit selfish. Relax. Have another drink.'

'No, I don't want any more. I think I've had too much already.'

'Nonsense.'

'I don't want any more,' she almost shouted it. 'I just want to go. It's too hot in here. I need some fresh air.' Her stomach churned and she leaned faintly against him. 'I need to lie down.'

He turned towards her and suddenly his grip relaxed as he murmured against her hair, 'Oh I get it. You crazy little idiot. Why on earth didn't you say?'

Hadn't she been doing just that, she thought dizzily, for the past hour? She waited as he said something to the rugger team. They laughed, slapped him on the back. She managed a half-hearted 'goodnight', wondering why they were all grinning like Cheshire cats and then, to her relief, they were out in the fresh air.

It hit her with the force of a jet stream and her knees buckled. 'I'm going to be sick.'

He backed off hastily. 'Oh no you're not! Just take a few deep breaths.'

She obeyed, feeling the cold air suck through her lungs like a knife. 'I still feel sick.'

He swore softly under his breath. Tears welled up in her eyes. He might have been just the littlest bit sympathetic. After all, it was his fault she was feeling sick. Come to think of it, it was his fault that the whole evening had been pretty much of a wash-out.

'Let's get to the car.' One arm was round her waist, his other hand was doing something to the buttons of her dress. She slapped it away.

'I'm not feeling faint, thank you.'

He seemed to find that funny. 'No, but we don't want you to feel restricted in any way, do we, my sweet. There's not an awful lot of room in my car.'

'Perhaps you ought to try getting a bigger one,' she snapped. 'Anyway, I can walk back to the Nurses' Home perfectly well. In fact I'd rather, then you can go back to your friends. I'm sure they must be missing you.'

'Oh I shouldn't think so. They know I'm likely to be kept fully occupied at least for the next hour, so they won't be looking for me.'

In the light reflected from the windows of the Main Block she saw his quick grin and for the first time felt the beginnings of panic as realisation began to dawn.

'Busy? Doing what exactly?' Her hands were against his chest now, as they reached the car, but he had manoeuvred her so that her back was pressed against the metal.

'Well that rather depends on you, my sweet.' His hand was on her thigh and Emma jumped.

'Don't do that.'

'Oh come on. You're not going to be a spoilsport.' His hand moved again and she felt her breath escape in a rush. This wasn't happening. It couldn't be.

'I really don't know what you're talking about. I just want to go home and be sick.' Her head was reeling as the drink combined with hunger and fresh air. 'Please, Phil, let me go.'

But his grip tightened. 'You're not really as naïve as you're making out, are you? You don't really expect me just to say goodnight and walk back, do you?'

She swallowed hard, wondering how on earth she had ever imagined he was attractive. 'Y—yes, as a matter of fact I do.'

'But the evening's young yet, my darling.' His face was close and she tried to wriggle away, feeling even more sick as the wave of alcohol on his breath as he tried to kiss her swept over her.

'I . . . I know, but I'm tired and I really do feel ill.' The strength seemed to be draining out of her legs. She tried to push him away but the effort was feeble and his hands hurt her arms. If he didn't let go soon she was going to be violently sick all over him. 'Please, Phil.'

But there was no understanding in his eyes as he pushed her back against the car. 'I'm not that crazy.

You don't seriously imagine I dragged you along here tonight just for the hell of it? Look, sweetie, I'll be honest, you're strictly not my type but what do you think it's going to do for my reputation if I go back there and have to admit I didn't get my money's worth?'

She gasped with shock. 'You don't mean . . . you don't meant this was just a . . . a dare?' Tears of anger pricked at her eyes and he laughed softly, brutally.

'Well what else? As I said, you're not my type, ordinarily, but as I always say,' his hand was inside the front of her dress, 'a change is as good as a rest.'

She struggled wildly, lashing out in what she soon knew was a losing battle. He was far stronger and she felt too sick and drained to retaliate. Perhaps if she passed out he would give up. The thought ran briefly through her head as she thwarted his exploring attempts with a sharply placed knee.

In a brief moment of triumph she heard him groan. It was short-lived. Anger merely seemed to give him momentum and she braced herself as he lunged at her again. She screamed as her dress tore but the sound was stifled by his jacket. She was going to faint. Not now, the thought hammered in her brain. For heaven's sake, not now.

And then, suddenly, she was fighting air. Her knees buckled and she sagged to the floor. Vaguely she was aware of Phil's voice, and another. There was something disturbingly familiar about it but her eyes wouldn't focus and she really felt past caring.

'If I were you, Carrington,' she heard the Senior Registrar's tone rap icily from somewhere above her, 'I'd get back to your so-called friends and try to sober up. You're a disgrace not only to your profession but to yourself. Now get out of my sight.'

From where she sat on the ground, Emma assumed that Phil went. There wasn't even a protest. Not that she really expected one. You didn't argue with a man like Garrard Blair, especially not when he was in a temper as he now seemed to be.

Conscious of the cold ground beneath her she tried to get to her feet, only to feel another wave of nausea overtake her so that she sank back, clutching feebly at the tear in her dress, her beautiful dress which had cost so much. Except that it didn't seem beautiful any more. She sobbed and carried on sobbing as she was suddenly lifted into a pair of arms which were so strong and magically warm that she didn't ever want them to let her go. She sighed and let her head droop against a jacket which smelled of expensive aftershave, then the Senior Registrar's voice brought her sharply back to reality.

'You crazy little fool. I warned you, but you wouldn't listen.'

If he had plunged her into a bath of cold water the effect couldn't have been more dramatic. She struggled to sit up and free herself, only to feel his grip tighten.

'For heaven's sake, keep still. I think you've caused quite enough trouble for one night.'

She gulped hard. 'I didn't cause any trouble . . .'

'Well you certainly went looking for it so you could hardly be surprised that you found it,' he snapped. 'Perhaps I should have left you to it.'

'Oh no.' She closed her eyes tightly and shuddered.

He didn't answer and she couldn't blame him, not when, even in her own eyes, she realised how it must have looked.

He whisked her effortlessly into the front seat of his car. It was only as she felt herself sink into the softly luxurious seats that she realised it *was* in fact his car, but before she could say anything, he had tucked a warm rug over her, and was going round to climb into the driving seat beside her.

If only her head wasn't aching so much and her stomach churning, she would actually quite enjoy the situation, she thought faintly, except that if her head wasn't aching, she wouldn't be here in the first place.

He started the engine and she sat up, too quickly. 'Where are you taking me?'

He didn't even glance in her direction as he swung the car out into the road and said curtly, 'Somewhere where you can get cleaned up and recover from your ordeal.' In the semi-darkness she saw him look at her now and felt the cold disapproval. 'I take it it *was* an ordeal. I didn't just step in at the wrong moment?'

She choked, furiously. 'Of course it was. You don't seriously imagine I invited his attentions, do you? Well certainly not that kind of attention,' she added lamely. He didn't answer. No doubt still drawing his own conclusions. She sat hunched back in the seat and removed a tear from her cheek with her tongue, hoping he wouldn't have noticed.

'I feel sick.'

Without a word he stopped the car and she flung the door open, promptly suiting actions to words. Her stomach heaved as it rid itself of the foul sherry and the gin, and a cool hand supported her burning head until the spasms passed. She felt like crying with humiliation and wretchedness. She would never be able to look him in the face again.

'You crazy little idiot. Don't you know better than to drink on an empty stomach?'

She slid back into the seat and closed her eyes. He was a beast. An arrogant, unsympathetic beast, and she hated him.

'There wasn't time to eat.' She thought longingly of the buffet and heard her stomach rumble, his ears were obviously as sharp as the rest of him.

'There was an excellent buffet.'

She ground her teeth at the note of condescension in his voice.

'Yes, well Phil was busy . . . talking to his friends.'

'And plying you with drinks, I don't doubt?' He changed gear savagely and the car purred along the road. Emma didn't answer. She felt too miserable and anyway it was absolutely none of his business.

She sat up, staring into the darkness. 'Where are we going? The Nurses' Home must be miles back.'

'I imagine it is,' he said dryly, concentrating on the road ahead. 'But you don't seriously expect me to take you back there looking like that?'

She hadn't thought about it until his gaze slid over her, leaving her in no doubt that she must be the unloveliest female he had ever had in his car.

'But where . . . ?'

'My flat isn't too far from here.'

She jumped. His flat? He couldn't be serious? 'But I can't go there.'

'I fail to see why not.' He frowned, taking his

eyes off the road for a moment. 'In any case I really don't see any alternative. I can just imagine the reception you'd get if you turned up looking like that. It might take some explaining and frankly I don't think it's the kind of thing that will do you or the image of St Clement's much good, do you?'

She scowled furiously at him in the darkness. She might have known he would cover up. No matter what his personal feelings about Phil Carrington or herself, he wasn't likely to want any scandal.

'I could have sneaked in. No one need have known.'

'You know better than that. In any case, you're hardly in a fit state.'

He was probably right. A dangerous state of lethargy was creeping over her. It must be the warmth of the car and the fact that her stomach had rid itself of the sherry. Her eyes flew open. 'But what about the dance? You can't just walk out like that. Your . . . your partner will be looking for you.'

'There's no problem,' he said airily. 'I had to get back anyway. I'm on duty in the morning so I had already said my goodbyes. Which is why I happened to be in the car-park at the appropriate time.'

She sank back, unable to think of a suitable answer and was dozing when the car slid quietly to a halt. Blinking hard she woke with a start and blushed as she realised that her head must have drooped against his shoulder. For a moment she let it rest there, hoping he wouldn't notice she was awake until he said blandly, 'We're here. Can you walk or shall I carry you?'

'Of course I can walk,' she snapped, too afraid of the emotions being carried by him might arouse. The car door swung open. She put her feet out and sagged at the knees with a gasp. Without a word he swept her up, manoeuvred a key into the front door and deposited her on a couch before switching on a lamp.

She stared round the room, taking in the large windows, hidden now as he drew across deep burgundy velvet drapes. The sofa on which she sat matched a large chair, it was deep and plush. On a coffee table books were scattered, there were more on the shelves—paintings on the walls. It was a masculine room, lacking the feminine touch but it was luxuriously comfortable. She didn't know why it should surprise her. After all, even Senior Registrars were human, and no doubt in time, if he could talk her into it—and she didn't doubt he would—the beautiful Miss Halston would soon put her own personal mark upon it.

She shivered and he knelt to put another log on the fire which blazed in the hearth.

'There's a bathroom through there.' He nodded in the direction. 'I suggest you get out of those things and take a shower. You'll find some pyjamas and a bathrobe in there. Not exactly elegant, and far too large I'm afraid, but they'll do while your own clothes dry out. The mud will probably brush off.'

She dragged her gaze from the gaping hole in the knee of her tights. She realised she was sitting, with her hands clasped about her, staring at him. Silhouetted against the fire his profile was sharply defined and his nearness was doing strange things to her. She couldn't move and her heart was thudding wildly.

Pyjamas? Surely he couldn't mean . . . ? Her voice wobbled crazily, 'I'm sure if I just clean up a bit I'll be fine, then if you wouldn't mind taking me back . . .'

His face darkened as he looked at her. 'Nurse Benedict, I assure you I have absolutely no intention of driving all the way back to St Clement's tonight, and especially at this hour.'

She stared at him. 'But . . . but you have to. I can . . . can't possibly stay here.' Her teeth were chattering, with cold as well as with some strange emotion. It was ridiculous the effect he was having on her and so were the tears which suddenly welled up and coursed down her cheeks. No, she certainly couldn't stay here.

'For heaven's sake.' He was on his feet now and he looked very angry. 'I promise you I have absolutely no designs upon your virtue if that's what you think, but I have no intention whatsoever of driving back to St Clement's tonight. I've had a long, hard day and I have an equally hard one tomorrow.'

She knew it was true. He was operating in the morning, but she couldn't speak.

'When did you last eat?' His voice was curt.

She shook her head. 'I can't remember. This morning . . .'

'I'll fix you an omelette and while I do so I suggest you get out of those clothes. Is that clear?'

He stared at her and his expression changed ominously as she didn't move. She couldn't move. Then, suddenly, with an explosive movement, his hands were on her arms and he had dragged her to her feet.

'For pity's sake, Emma, don't look like that.'

She closed her eyes, not knowing what he meant and scarcely caring. The only thing she was conscious of was his nearness and the fact that she longed to be kissed. It was crazy, utterly crazy, but suddenly his mouth came down on hers. The kiss was long and hard and brutal, and for a few seconds she couldn't move. Then, as a wave of desire surged through her, her hands rose, her lips parted and she felt herself drawn closer until her body was taut against his, and when he released her abruptly, she was trembling.

She stared at him, scarcely able to breathe let alone speak, wishing only that the kiss had gone on for ever. There was a long silence, broken only by the crackling of the fire. She was trembling violently, and knew that if he reached out for her again then she would go into his arms and stay there. Knew also that she was in love with him and that it was quite hopeless.

He spoke abruptly. 'Go and have that shower and get changed. I'll have your food ready by the time you've finished, then you can get some sleep.'

Her eyes widened, and as if he had interpreted her thoughts he said sharply, 'Go to bed, Emma. There's no need to worry, I have every intention of sleeping here on the couch. It will all be perfectly proper and I'll see to it that you get back to the hospital in time in the morning.'

She stared at him, not wanting it all to be perfectly proper. Not caring. 'But I . . .'

'I said go to bed, before I do something we'll both

regret.' His voice thundered with such anger that she turned and fled without another word.

She undressed, showered quickly between sobs, and sat on the bed, huddled in a bathrobe which was far too big, staring at her bare toes in utter misery.

'I wouldn't have regretted anything,' she muttered, wiping a tear from the corner of her mouth. 'I wouldn't have regretted it at all. But *he* would.' The thought hammered cruelly. He would because he was still in love with the girl who jilted him.

Much later, as she lay in the large bed, wrapped in his pyjamas, she wondered how she was ever going to be able to stay at St Clement's after this, knowing how she felt.

It was a long time before she fell asleep, still without having resolved the situation.

CHAPTER TWELVE

THE CAR drew up at traffic lights and Emma broke the silence without looking at the man beside her.

'You could drop me here, please. The Nurses' Home is only just around the corner. I have to go to my room to change into uniform.' She looked down at the dress she was wearing and stifled a grimace of distaste. In the cold light of day it looked . . . well, she didn't think she would ever wear it again.

His expression didn't change. 'I'm not in the habit of dropping people off, Nurse Benedict. I'm quite capable of delivering you to the doorstep.' He frowned, glancing at his watch and she noticed the tiny, dark hairs on his arm. 'You're cutting it a bit fine as it is, and I don't imagine you want to incur Sister's wrath.'

The car eased out of the main stream of traffic and round the corner. Emma stared nervously up the large Victorian block which was the Nurses' Home and hoped no one was looking. The mere thought of what the hospital grapevine would make of this was beyond thinking on, but if the thought had crossed his own mind, Garrard Blair gave no sign of it.

The car drew to a halt and he leaned across to open the door. She leapt out before the scent of his aftershave could get to her.

'Thanks. I really am grateful . . . for what you

did. I hope . . .' she floundered, 'I hope it doesn't cause you any problems.'

The dark brows furrowed slightly. 'I don't anticipate any, Nurse Benedict.' He glanced at his watch. 'If I were you I'd hurry. You have about ten minutes to get on to the ward, unless you want Sister on the war-path.'

The sudden formality swept the smile from her face and she stepped back to stare after him as the car pulled away, leaving her standing on the pavement outside the Nurses' Home. Was it possible that this was the man who had actually kissed her last night? Whose bed she had slept in, albeit alone?

She turned and made her way slowly up the steps and to her room where she changed into uniform. Looking in the mirror as she fastened her cap, her face looked pale and there were shadows under her eyes. How different from the way she had looked last night. But then, that was last night. Today everything was back to normal, back to reality. Perhaps she had been a fool to think that anything could have been changed by a single kiss.

Sighing heavily she fastened the belt round her waist. How was she going to be able to stay at St Clement's, loving Garrard Blair, seeing him every day? A tap at the door brought her sharply out of the reverie and Sue came in looking crossly anxious.

'Oh thank heavens. Where have you been? I knocked ages ago but you didn't answer. I thought you'd overslept.'

Emma quickly gathered up her cape, hoping to

hide the sudden flushing of her cheeks as she did so. 'Thanks anyway. I'm ready.'

Sue looked at her. 'You look awful. How did it go last night? I looked for you but there was such a crush and we were a bit late getting there.'

Emma made a fuss of tucking her hair under her cap. 'As a matter of fact I didn't enjoy it particularly.' She managed to laugh. 'Not really my scene.' She made for the door but Sue was still sitting on the bed, watching her with a frown.

'You really are all right?'

'Yes, of course,' she muttered crossly. 'Why shouldn't I be? Oh hell, come on, I don't fancy getting a ticking off from Sister the minute I walk on to the ward.' She raced off down the corridor, Sue following almost at running pace as they crossed towards the Main Block and headed for the stairs.

'How come I didn't see you?' Sue skipped aside to let a white-coated figure pass.

'I left early.'

There was a moment's silence. 'Don't tell me you went back to Phil's place. Oh you didn't?'

'No, I didn't.' Emma's mouth compressed firmly. 'Look, I really don't want to go into details, not now.' Not ever, she thought and brushed a hand against her head. It was throbbing and she wished she had taken a couple of aspirins.

'You look awful.'

'Thanks.'

Sue pushed the swing doors and stopped, her face anxious. 'I was worried you know. I mean, I knocked on your door last night and when you didn't answer I thought perhaps you were asleep but this morning . . . well I knocked again and looked in . . . and you weren't there.' There was a slight flush to her face. 'Look, I don't want to pry but . . . well, I mean, I know what Phil Carrington's reputation is.'

Emma bit her lip. 'Honestly you don't need to worry. I'm not a complete fool. As a matter of fact we had a row, in the car-park of all places. It was my fault, I'd had too much to drink, so had he. Anyway we . . . we parted company.' She hurried through the door, heading for the ward. 'Look there really isn't anything to tell.'

'But where on earth did you spend the night? I was worried sick.'

Emma stopped in her tracks and swallowed hard. 'As it happened the Senior Registrar came along just as things were getting a bit nasty. He sent Phil on his way and . . . well I was in a pretty sorry state so he took me to his place and cleaned me up and I spent the night there because it was too late to come back here. That's all there was to it.'

Sue was staring at her, wide-eyed with disbelief. 'You mean, you actually spent the night with Garrard Blair?'

'Not *with* him,' Emma snapped. 'Well, not like that.' Her shoes squeaked as she quickened her steps. 'It was all perfectly innocent. I slept on the bed. He slept on the couch. It was hardly romantic, especially not after I'd been sick all over him, so don't go making a mountain out of a molehill.'

Sue looked at her doubtfully. 'Well I hope you can convince the hospital grapevine of that.'

Emma stared at her. 'What do you mean?'

'Well, you know what it's like. If the slightest

breath should get out, it doesn't matter how innocent . . .'

'But I don't see how it could. It isn't possible.'

'I just hope you're right, otherwise they're going to have a field day.' She looked at her watch. 'Oh lor, we've got one minute.' She raced up the stairs, taking them two at a time, leaving Emma to stand watching, a look of dawning horror on her face.

Suddenly it wasn't herself she was worried about. It was the Senior Registrar. The last thing he was likely to take kindly to was having his name linked with any kind of scandal, especially not with a mere first-year nurse, and certainly not if he was still in love with Sir James Halston's daughter.

Somehow, though she was never sure how, she managed to get through the next few hours. For once it was a relief to be so busy that she scarcely had time to breathe let alone think. There was something vastly comforting about the familiar routine, even though her heart hammered violently every time a figure in a white coat came through the ward doors.

This is ridiculous, she told herself firmly, as she bent over a bed straightening the covers. I've got to snap out of it. Or perhaps I'd better start thinking seriously about moving to a different job, a new area altogether.

It was a depressing thought. She liked St Clement's, but it was going to be impossible to work here when the mere thought of coming face to face with Garrard Blair seemed to turn her legs to jelly.

'Nurse.' Sister emerged from the office and raised a beckoning hand. 'I've just had a call to say that Mr Squires will be coming back to us some time today.'

'Oh that's marvellous, Sister. He must be getting better.'

'It certainly means he has made sufficient progress to give reason to hope, Nurse,' Sister agreed, quietly. 'We shall need to have a bed made ready.'

'Mr Lawson is being discharged this morning, Sister.'

'Good, then as soon as possible have the bed stripped and remade. I imagine Mr Squires will be moved later this morning and Mr Blair will be in to see him this afternoon. Make sure all the notes are to hand, Nurse. *All* the notes.'

'Yes, Sister.' Emma clenched and unclenched her hands behind her back. It wasn't going to be as easy as she had hoped to avoid seeing him again, not on a busy ward like Men's Surgical. Her hands shook as she helped Staff Nurse Blake to change a dressing and Staff looked at her sharply.

'Are you all right, Nurse?'

'Y . . . yes, Staff.'

'Well you don't look it.' Staff tutted crossly. 'I suppose you went to the dance last night.'

It was more statement than question and Emma nodded. 'Yes, Staff.'

'I thought so. And what time did you roll into bed this morning? Really, you nurses should have a greater sense of responsibility.'

Emma's hand jerked convulsively and a steel dish clattered to the floor. She pressed a hand to her head and bent to pick up the dish which was revolving noisily as staff rapped furiously, 'Leave it, Nurse. Go and fetch another and when this dressing is finished you had better take your coffee break and get yourself sorted out. A couple of aspirins will do wonders for a hangover.'

Emma fled to fetch the dish, Staff's words ringing in her ears. She paused, breathing hard and fighting back the tears.

It was a relief to be able to escape to the cafeteria, and even more so to find a table which was empty. Though her relief was short-lived as Sally walked in and spotted her.

'Hi.' She came across, put her coffee down and slid into the empty seat. 'You don't mind if I join you, only I hate sitting alone.' She spooned sugar into her cup and leaned forward, conspiratorially. 'What's this I've been hearing about you, then?'

Emma's glance shot upwards. 'Hearing? I don't know what you mean.'

Sally chuckled. 'Well I'm not surprised. I laughed like a drain when I heard it, but there's some sort of crazy story going around that you actually spent the night with the Senior Registrar and—can you imagine it, of all the crazy things— that you were seen rolling up at the Nurses' Home this morning in his car, as large as life.'

Emma gulped her coffee, feeling it scald its way down her throat as her scalp suddenly grew taut with horror. 'Just where did you hear it?'

'Oh it's everywhere. Well, well on its way.' Sally screwed up her eyes in a frown of concentration. 'Someone in Women's Med told me first thing, and I heard it again in Cas. I should think it's over the entire hospital by now. You know how these things spread.'

Emma groaned. Someone, and she could guess who, certainly hadn't wasted any time. Phil must have gone straight back to the dance and poured a tale of injured woe into the ears of the luscious Staff Nurse Peach, who had been only too ready to make the most of it. But if the news had already reached Women's Med, how long before it reached Garrard Blair's ears? Emma covered her face with her hands and the grin on Sally's face gradually faded.

'For heaven's sake, it's not true? Is it?'

Emma couldn't meet her friend's wide-eyed gaze. She shook her head. 'It really wasn't the way everyone seems determined to make it sound,' she thrust defensively, and knew that her cheeks were blazing. 'He brought me back to the Nurses' Home, that's all.'

'It *is* true.'

Emma almost leapt to her feet to stifle her friend's cry of incredulity. 'No, it isn't.'

'You mean he didn't take you back to his place and you didn't spend the night together?'

'No . . . yes.' She clasped a hand against her aching head. 'It wasn't like that. It was all perfectly innocent, I promise you. He just happened to rescue me from what could have been a rather nasty situation, and I couldn't get back so it seemed easier to spend the night at his place. He slept on the couch. And that's precisely what did happen, I swear it.'

Sally's gaze of incredulity became a grin. 'My dear girl, I believe you, but you're going to have a hard time persuading anyone else. There's not a female walking these hallowed corridors who wouldn't give her eye teeth to spend the night with our gorgeous Garrard Blair, but he's never as much as looked at any of them, and now this.'

'What do you mean, "this"?' Emma squeaked. 'Anyway, he was supposed to have been engaged to Sir James Halston's daughter.'

'Oh that.' Sally shrugged. 'There was some talk. I heard it was all off. Not that you ever know with the grapevine.'

'Well I can assure you he's in love with her and he's not going to like it if a story like this gets out.'

Sally's laughter faded as she saw the look of misery on her friend's face. 'Look, I do believe you. God knows it's difficult to imagine how . . .' She broke off with a sigh of exasperation. 'Well you have to admit, he's gorgeous. If he as much as looked at me I'd fall at his feet.'

'I wouldn't recommend it,' Emma said dryly, closing her eyes on the memory of being swept up into those arms. 'What on earth am I going to do? Apart from leave St Clem's by the first stage?'

'I don't see what you can do. By now they've probably got you engaged and half-way down the aisle. Someone even told me that it had been going on secretly for months.'

'Oh no!'

'Look, don't take it so seriously. It will all have blown over in a few weeks when they find something and someone else to talk about.'

'*Weeks!* I may not live that long if he gets to hear about it.'

'You mean when, not if. He's bound to.' Sally eyed her, shrewdly. 'Perhaps you'd better get to him first, if you're really sure he's going to be as mad as you say.'

'How could he not be?'

'Well, I've no idea. You two really do seem to strike sparks off one another, don't you?'

'You could say that. I can't help feeling I've lit an entire volcano this time.' She got to her feet. 'I wonder if I should offer Sister my resignation now or later.'

'Later? What later?' Sally ducked as a screwed up paper napkin sailed past her head. 'Well, best of luck.'

'I think I'm going to need it.'

Emma felt her pulse quickening. If only she hadn't gone to the dance last night. If only she hadn't gone with Phil. If only she had never set eyes on the Senior Registrar . . .

CHAPTER THIRTEEN

SHE was late getting off duty. It had been a busy morning. Sister had had to go to a meeting and because of an emergency admission, by the time the patient had been settled and she had exchanged a few words with young Alan Squires as well, it was nearly half-past one before she had finally left the ward. Not that she would have minded as a rule. Half-days were fine in summer when you could lounge around on the lawn at the back of the Nurses' Home, or wander into the nearby town, but today it was raining heavily, with a promise of snow in the air, and anyway, there was something else she had to do before she could go off.

Wrapping her cape round her she walked down the stairs and over to Outpatients. Head bent, deep in thought, she was musing over the definite signs of improvement in Alan Squires and almost wished it had been her afternoon on so that she could have seen the pleasure on his fiancée's face when she arrived at visiting time. But that was one of the things you learned in nursing, there were the good moments and the bad. You simply had to take satisfaction from knowing that the patient was going to get better.

Outpatients was quiet, probably because it was early yet. The afternoon clinic didn't start until two o'clock, although a number of patients were sitting waiting, thumbing through a pile of magazines.

Emma smiled as she walked past the reception desk and along a corridor, finally coming to a halt outside a door. Her heart thudded as her hand rose to knock. She couldn't do it. She couldn't possibly face him, not to see the terrible contempt in his eyes. Yet what was the alternative? To let him hear the things that were being said from someone else?

Her hand hung, poised in mid-air. What if he had already heard the talk and assumed that it was she who had started it? No, he couldn't possibly. But it was a risk she couldn't take. He had a right to know. After which . . . she had already made up her mind. She was going to hand in her notice and leave St Clement's as quickly as possible.

She tapped quietly at the door and for a moment a feeling of relief swept through her as no one answered. He was out. The evil hour could be postponed. She had already turned away when the door opened and he was standing there, a look of surprise on his face whilst she stood rooted to the spot, her mouth open.

He frowned. It was strange she hadn't noticed before how his hair curled against the collar of his white coat, or how dark the lashes were that fringed his eyes.

'Did you want to see me?'

She jumped, swallowing convulsively. 'Oh no . . . that is . . . well, yes.'

He didn't move. 'I have a clinic in about fifteen minutes. Is it urgent?'

Now was the time to be a coward and back out. 'Well, it is rather.'

He paused then stepped back into the office. She

followed, staring at the desk covered with books and papers.

'Not in trouble with Sister are you? I didn't get you back too late?'

If only it were that simple. Her face turned up to his and he saw the faint colour steal into it, the fear, and wondered what had caused it. 'N-no, nothing like that.' He was waiting, but how on earth did she say it? Did she even want to when it meant that she would have to see the anger slowly fill his eyes, feel the humiliation.

'I shouldn't have come.' She half-turned towards the door but his voice stopped her as he said calmly,

'But you did, Emma, so hadn't you better tell me whatever it is that's troubling you?' The shrewd eyes watched her and saw the frown which etched its way into her forehead before her fingers rose to push a strand of hair beneath her cap.

'I . . . I don't know how to start.'

'The beginning is usually the best place, I find.' His voice was surprisingly gentle, almost too gentle. She closed her eyes then opened them quickly as he said from much closer, 'It can't really be that bad can it, Emma?'

His use of her name filled her with unutterable depression. 'Oh you've no idea.' It would have been easier if he had been angry. 'It's awful. I suppose I should have realised . . . but I didn't. I just didn't imagine . . .' She hated the tears which were suddenly coursing down her cheeks as he came slowly towards her.

'What are you talking about, Emma? Just take a deep breath and calm down and tell me.' His hands were on her arms. She wished he hadn't touched her because it sent shivers down her spine.

'Surely you must have heard?' For some reason she began to feel angry. 'It's all over the hospital. How can you not have heard?'

His expression was amazingly placid. 'My dear Emma, I don't listen to gossip. Blow your nose. Here, let me.' To her chagrin he used his own handkerchief as if she were a child and she snatched it away crossly.

'Don't do that, I'm not a child.'

His mouth twitched slightly. 'No, you're not, are you, Emma?'

She didn't stop to wonder what he meant. 'Everyone's talking about it.'

Dark brows rose. 'Well in that case it must be very serious.'

'Yes, yes it is.' If only he would stop looking at her like that. 'Don't you even care?'

'What precisely is it that I'm supposed to care about, Emma?'

She stifled a scream of impatience. 'But they're saying . . . they're saying that you . . . I . . . we spent the night together.' Her cheeks flamed scarlet and a gasp left her parted lips as he said calmly,

'But we did.'

It couldn't be true, she thought, dizzily. He was just standing there as calmly as if nothing had happened.

'Yes but . . . you know what I mean. They're implying that we . . .'

'That we weren't exactly innocent, you mean?' Was he laughing at her? She looked up at him from beneath her thick lashes, defying him to do so, but no, he wasn't laughing. In fact he looked very serious. Her face whitened.

'I tried to put a stop to it but it just seems to have made things worse.'

He frowned. 'Yes, I imagine it might.' She had the impression that he wasn't even really listening. 'The grapevine gets hold of something and it's hard to stop.' He looked at her. 'I'm sorry, Emma. I didn't intend that you should be subjected to anything like this.'

'Oh but . . . I'm not . . . I mean, it wasn't myself I was thinking of,' she stammered. 'I simply realised how awkward it would make things for you and I thought perhaps it might not be too late to do something about it.' She looked away from him and stared down at her shoes before heading slowly for the door. 'I shall hand in my notice, of course.'

Suddenly his face was grim as he looked at her. 'Give in your notice? But why? I don't see the necessity.'

'Well you must see that I can't possibly stay. Not now.' She backed instinctively closer to the door as he moved towards her. He came to a halt and his face was very angry as he loomed over her.

'Perhaps you had better explain to me, Emma. Just what are you running away from?'

'But . . . the scandal.'

His mouth twisted. 'Don't you know that hospital gossip is a five-minute wonder.' He had reached out and was holding her now, his mouth so close that she had only to raise her face. She kept it lowered stubbornly. 'In any case there's a perfectly logical answer.'

Her head jerked up and as if he had been waiting

for it his mouth descended possessively over hers. Her body was rigid with shock and confusion, then she moaned softly as her mouth responded, traitorously. I'm so weak, she thought. Thoroughly spineless.

'There is?' she murmured when he released her.

'But of course. There's only one way to put a stop to idle gossip. We simply announce that we are engaged. I think that should do it, don't you?'

She was glad the door was behind her or she would have fallen. She had to look at him to see if he was joking—if so it was a very cruel joke. 'You're not serious?'

He sighed very softly. 'My dear Emma, you seem to have a habit of doubting my integrity. Why is that?'

She stared at her feet. 'I've no idea. I don't intend to make you feel that.'

'And yet you succeed admirably. I'm hardly likely to joke about something so serious.'

He might at least show some enthusiasm, she thought, instead of behaving as if he was making a business arrangement. Or perhaps he was doing just that. Her heart suddenly felt like lead.

'It really isn't necessary.'

She waited, breathlessly, for him to say that he loved her. Instead he said with a slight smile, 'I presume you like diamonds? Aren't they supposed to be a girl's best friend?'

'I wouldn't know. I've never had any. Diamonds I mean.'

His mouth contorted slightly. 'Then we'll have to change that won't we? Diamonds it is. I'll see to it. I imagine I can find something suitable but if not I'm sure we can change it.'

He didn't even ask her if it was all right. He looked at his watch and frowned and she felt as if the interview was at an end. 'I'll pick you up about eight tonight, is that convenient? We can go out and celebrate.'

Her numbed lips moved but it took a great effort to prise them apart. Where were all the feelings she had imagined she would feel when this moment arrived? It should have been the happiest moment of her life and yet she simply felt a terrible awareness that something was missing, that none of this was real.

'I really don't think . . .' She swallowed hard. 'Look, we can't just get engaged like this. It's . . . well it's ridiculous. We don't even . . . I mean . . .'

His expression didn't change and yet she sensed that he had withdrawn suddenly, that some kind of barrier had come down between them.

'We don't love each other, is that what you're trying to say?' He turned away, gathering some papers from his desk in a brisk movement so that his face was hidden. 'You're right, of course, but then, since the sole purpose of the exercise is to put an end to the gossip, it's hardly relevant is it? We simply need to appear engaged for a suitable period, after which we simply call it off and you can make whatever announcement you think appropriate. It will be a seven-day wonder and then the grapevine will find something else to talk about. It always does.'

She turned blindly for the door. 'I have to go.'

'I'll pick you up tonight.'

She nodded and ran, aware only of the bitter irony of the situation. His only concern was to safeguard her reputation and yet she would have sacrificed it willingly in return for his love.

He was waiting as she came down the steps. The door of the sleek, black car was opened and she hesitated. It wasn't too late to turn back, even now.

'Get in.' His tone was peremptory. She still hesitated, then out of the corner of her eye she saw a crowd of nurses just coming off duty, crossing from the Main Block. She got in and he started the engine.

'You look very nice.'

He was being kind, she thought. Admittedly the soft, blue woollen dress was particularly flattering and she had taken endless pains with her hair and make-up, but she was still aware that no matter what she did she wasn't likely to compare with the kind of woman he was used to.

In fact she had spent half the afternoon alternating between tears and debating whether to ring him and tell him she couldn't go through with it after all. In the end sheer cowardice had prevented her. She didn't doubt that if she had done so he would probably have come looking for her anyway. There was his own reputation to safeguard too, she thought bitterly, and so had finally run a bath and soaked in flower-scented water until some of the tensions had begun to edge away.

The only trouble was they returned now with a vengeance as she sat beside him, more conscious than ever of the darkly handsome profile and the strong hands on the wheel. She drew back into the seat, wrapping her misery round her like a cloak, wondering how long he considered 'an appropriate period of time' to be. Days, weeks, months?

'You're very quiet, Emma. Is anything wrong?'

'No, I've just had a bad day that's all,' she said evasively. 'I'm in Sister's bad books again.'

'Oh dear, what did you do. Send the wrong patient up to theatre?'

She cast him a withering look. 'Even *I'm* not that bad. As a matter of fact I gave a blanket bath to a patient who was perfectly capable of going to the bathroom and he didn't say a word.' She blushed and thought she heard a soft chuckle escape him.

'Is that all? I expect he enjoyed every minute of it.'

'Oh, I'm sure he did. Unfortunately Sister wasn't at all amused and I got a long lecture on keeping my mind on my work.'

'Isn't your mind on your work, then?'

She turned her head away, pretending to stare out of the window. 'I was trying to decide what to wear tonight, if you must know,' she lied.

'Well you made the right choice, you look absolutely delightful. I like your hair like that. It suits you.'

She hated him for being so nice. What was the point when he was going to break her heart anyway?

'I thought we'd go to an Italian restaurant I know. You do like Italian food?'

'I love it.' It would all taste like chaff anyway.

'Good, so do I. It's just a small place but the food is first-class.'

He was right, she had to admit, as they sat at a table and were served with huge dishes of spaghetti and meat in a rich sauce, subtly flavoured with garlic. At any other time she would have enjoyed it enormously but tonight every mouthful was an ordeal as she sat there, trying not to be aware of him every time she looked up and saw him silhouetted against a brilliant halo of light from the candles.

He refilled her glass and her hand shook as she raised it to her lips. 'It won't do any harm,' he said. 'At least you've eaten this time, if not very much.' He looked at her plate. 'Are you sure you're feeling all right?'

'Yes, fine. I'm just not very hungry, that's all.'

The door opened, letting in a draught of cool air as a small group came in laughing and talking.

She jumped as his hand closed over hers where it rested on the table-cloth. 'There's no need to look so terrified, Emma. I meant it, you know, when I said that this arrangement of ours was purely a matter of convenience. That is what you want, isn't it?'

He was watching her closely, anxiously. Probably afraid that she would say she had been compromised and demand that he make an honest woman of her, she thought, freeing her hand and wrestling with a piece of spaghetti on her fork. 'Yes, of course it is.'

His eyes narrowed. 'Well in that case . . .' He reached into his pocket and produced a small box. 'I think you had better have this. Just to make things official. I hope you like it.'

Like it? She couldn't avoid a gasp of sheer delight as he slid a perfect, single diamond on to her finger.

If she had chosen it herself—not that she would have of course, because she guessed it must have cost a fortune—it was exactly what she would have wanted. It felt strange and heavy on her finger and she stared at it as he held her hand, the stone catching and reflecting the candle flames. She couldn't speak, the lump in her throat was too large and utterly immovable.

'Is it all right?' He frowned. 'I can always change it.'

'Oh no, no.' She drew her hand back quickly and thought, why bother to change it when we both know this is one diamond that isn't for ever. 'It's perfect.'

His hand tightened over hers. 'I'm glad you're pleased and I do believe you're actually blushing.'

Her gaze flickered warily in the direction of the far corner. 'I've just realised that the crowd who came in are from the hospital and they're watching.'

He didn't look away from her. Instead he leaned across the table, pushing the candle away, and before she could protest he was kissing her firmly on the lips. She felt as if she was floating on a cloud, then he released her and she came back to earth with a bump to hear him say, 'That should give them something to talk about, I think, don't you?'

She forced a smile, her lips rigid as she fought not to cry. Yes, undoubtedly it would give them something to talk about. The pity was that they would all be wrong. Her other hand turned the ring on her finger. It was beautiful yet cold as ice. Like his feelings for her.

'Come on, I'll take you home.'

It was a miserable end to what might, under different circumstances, have been the most marvellous evening of her life.

CHAPTER FOURTEEN

For the next few days Emma seemed to be walking round in a dream. She came off duty feeling exhausted, fell into bed only to find that she spent hours tossing and turning, and woke in the mornings feeling completely drained.

Normally she would have looked forward to a day off, spending the time doing odd chores, having a lie in, taking a leisurely bath and generally doing as she pleased. But for once she had had to escape and had spent the whole day just wandering around the shops, not even buying anything except a perfectly useless ornament. Anything rather than have to face the inevitable barrage of questions and congratulations which had caught up with her finally.

She didn't think she would ever be able to forgive him for the little charade in the restaurant. She had known of course that the grapevine would get to work, but not that it would do so with quite such speed or relish. She had hardly set foot through the main doors next morning before it started. Harry was the first, greeting her with a broad wink and a knowing look.

'I knew it,' he wheezed. 'Allus said the best gets snapped up 'fore I gets a look in. Still, congratulations, Nurse. He's a nice looking fellah, knows what's what too.' Harry tapped the side of his nose. 'You'll be all right with that one. 'Course there's lots as will be green but don't you pay 'em no mind.

Just send me a piece of weddin' cake and don't you go lettin' 'im persuade you to leave too soon. This old place won't be the same without you.'

It was quite a speech and she stood listening, wishing herself miles away. If only he knew. 'I don't think there's much danger of that, Harry. Anyway, our plans are a little unsettled yet.' She winced at the understatement then looked at her watch. 'Heavens, is that the time. I'd better rush if I'm not going to get another black mark.' She fled and made her way on to the ward to be hit at once by an atmosphere which sent her spirits plunging.

She saw Sue casting one of her 'I must talk to you' glances in her direction and stifled a groan. Surely the word couldn't have got around already? But then she might have guessed that something like that wouldn't remain secret for very long, especially after Garrard Blair had gone out of his way to make sure it didn't.

Her colour rose as she remembered that kiss and she clamped her lips shut, tightly. Blast the man, she thought fiercely, swallowing tears. He had absolutely no right to play around with other people's lives.

She filed into Sister's office with the rest of the staff to hear the Kardex read, glad, for once, that it offered no opportunity for chat. Sister's voice merged somewhere into the background as her thoughts took over and she wondered, bleakly, as she stared out of the window, why she had had to fall in love with that man of all men.

She sighed deeply and became aware of Sister Meredith's gaze as it rose frostily to fix itself upon her.

'Am I boring you, Nurse Benedict?'

Emma started, blushing a deep pink. 'N . . . no, Sister.'

'Good, I'm glad to hear it.' Sister's gaze lingered for a moment, taking in the pale face and shadowed eyes, she seemed about to say something else then changed her mind. 'Right.' She rose to her feet. 'Let's get on with it then, shall we?'

They all trooped to the door like obedient sheep until Sister's voice halted Emma in her tracks.

'Wait a moment, Nurse Benedict. I'd like a word with you please.'

Heart thudding, Emma turned and stood with her hands clasped behind her. 'Yes, Sister.'

But Sister waited until the door was closed before she sat at her desk, clasped her hands together and said briskly, 'I gather we may be losing you soon, Nurse. I'm sorry to hear it. Given time I think you may have proved to be a credit, not only to this ward but to St Clement's.'

Emma stared, wondering if she had actually heard the words, and Laura Meredith smiled.

'Yes, I'm sure there must have been times when both of us have doubted it, but I've watched you fairly closely and there has been a gradual but definite improvement in your attitude to your work.'

'Thank you, Sister.' Emma beamed, her voice breathless with pleasure.

Sister wasn't looking at her. 'I would be sorry to think you might leave nursing altogether once you are married.' The shrewd gaze rose. 'Of course being the wife of a registrar won't be easy, though your experience with us is bound to stand you in good stead.' Emma stood grimly silent. 'But I would like to think that you might feel able to return to us some day, to finish your training and put to use the knowledge you have already acquired.'

Emma concentrated her gaze on the desk rather than the figure behind it. Behind her back her hands were clenched so tightly that she felt the nails bite into her palms. 'I wouldn't want to give up my nursing completely, Sister. I'm just not very sure . . . I don't know . . .' Her voice broke off.

'Well I'm glad to hear it. Good nurses are hard to come by. We lose far too many to marriage but I shall take a personal pride in thinking that the things we have taught you will not be completely wasted.' Her face beamed in kindly concern, unaware of the knife she was innocently twisting. 'Mr Blair is a fine man, an excellent surgeon. I'm sure you must be very happy in the knowledge that you will be able to help him in his career.'

Emma felt a dull throbbing in her head and knew she couldn't go through with it—all the congratulations, facing the questions and knowing all the time that it was nothing more than lies and pretence.

'Yes I . . . I am very proud, Sister. I'm just not very sure yet when I shall be leaving or what my plans are.' Well that at least was true, she thought. The only certain thing was that she couldn't stay at St Clement's now.

'Well that's perfectly understandable.' Sister became briskly efficient again. 'As soon as you do know perhaps you'll come and let me know. And now I suggest you get on with your work. We still have a busy ward to run.'

'Yes, Sister.' She headed for the door and purposely kept her head down, avoiding Sue's glance in her direction as she made her way down the ward. Her fingers strained to the ring, worn on a chain beneath her uniform. Jewellery wasn't permitted but in any case she couldn't have brought herself to wear it. It would be too humiliating, too painful a reminder of her feelings. No, she drew herself up sharply, the sooner this farce was ended the better.

As luck would have it the morning passed in a busy round which left little time for anything but the tasks in hand. She moved mechanically, yet still somehow managing to find time for the necessary chats with patients who needed company or reassurance. Beds were stripped and remade, lockers were swabbed, drinks and medicines handed out, dressings changed. By lunch time she was feeling drained and tense and it was a relief when Sister told her to go for lunch. Looking at her watch she was amazed to find that the time had flown. It was even more of a relief, she found herself thinking, when Sue was asked to take her own lunch later so that she wouldn't have to answer the inevitable questions for a while yet at least.

Contrary to all training and lectures in PTS which instilled into nurses the need for eating proper meals, she bolted a sandwich in the cafeteria, drained a cup of coffee and hurried back to the ward. Luckily Sister was too busy to notice that she had taken only half her allocated hour and sent Sue off with a rejoinder not to be late getting back.

'We have a full list to get through and Mr Blair does his round at two.'

Emma felt the sweat break out on her palms and knew she couldn't face him. The mere thought of him walking through the doors, the possibility that he would expect her to keep up appearances was too much.

She managed to keep her face an impassive mask as Sister motioned her to one of the beds in the far corner of the ward. 'Mr Simpkin is due back from theatre any time now, Nurse, make sure you keep an eye on him, and Mr Davison has had his pre-med. The porters will take him up when they bring Mr Simpkins back to the ward.' She looked at her watch. 'Mr Carter is due for his pre-med in about half an hour. I have to go to a meeting which means Staff will be in charge. We're going to be a bit short-handed for a while so you'll probably find yourself trotting up to theatre several times.'

'That's all right, Sister, I don't mind.' In fact, she thought, it would be a good opportunity to get away from the ward, if only briefly.

There was no visiting on Men's Surgical that afternoon. It was one of the busiest operating days and visitors came in the evening instead, which meant that the day seemed particularly long to those patients who were post-op, and there was a general air of boredom and gloom which the nurses did their best to dispel.

Emma crossed the ward to look at the man who had just come back from theatre. He was still sleeping and would be allowed to do so until he woke naturally. She made the routine checks, filled in the chart and moved to the next bed where Mr Davison was drowsily unworried now that his pre-med was beginning to take effect.

'Hullo, Mr Davison, how are you feeling? A little woozy?' He opened his eyes and grinned at her.

'Like I drank a whole bottle of whisky, Nurse.'

'Well that's fine.' She couldn't help smiling. 'You'll be going up to theatre soon. I'll go with you and when you wake up again you'll be back in the ward and it will all be over.'

He closed his eyes again and at that precise moment the doors opened and the porters appeared with the trolley. She waited as they lifted him carefully from the bed, then walked beside him as the trolley was wheeled down the ward, and held his hand when it seemed his newly-found confidence momentarily weakened. The porters talked and joked quietly with him and she joined in.

'Don't worry, Mr Davison, we'll save tea for you for when you come back. You may wish we hadn't.' She heard him chuckle softly. 'Don't worry now. I'm right here. We're just going up in the lift to theatre.'

The ward doors opened seconds before the trolley reached them. Emma, concentrating on seeing that it was manoeuvred through, was only half aware of the tall, dark-suited figure pressed against the doors as they passed through. It was only as she murmured 'thank you' that her gaze happened to flicker upwards and she felt her body go rigid as a voice responded quietly,

'That's all right, Emma, I'll see you when you get back.'

For an instant her heart leapt as she looked up into Garrard's face. He smiled but somehow her own mouth didn't respond. It felt too frozen, then without a word she charged after the trolley, knowing that he was staring after her. But she couldn't help it. She had known she would have to see him some time or other, it was inevitable, but nothing had prepared her for the effect it would have on her.

She moved blindly towards the lift. The doors slid open and she entered and stood beside the trolley, waiting as the doors closed again, but not before she had seen the look of annoyance on Garrard's face.

There was no time to think about it, however. The lift moved up to the top floor where the operating theatres were. It was strange how often people expected them to be downstairs and talked of 'going down' to theatre.

She stepped out of the lift, glancing at her patient as he was wheeled out. With a bit of luck, if the lists were running to schedule, Mr Davison would soon be back on the ward, sleeping peacefully and minus the pain which a long-nurtured hernia had been causing him.

She was about to make her way back to the ward, using the stairs since nurses weren't permitted to use lifts which might be required for moving patients, when one of the theatre staff waylaid her.

'Ah, Nurse,' Staff Nurse Latimer looked slightly harassed. 'Are you from Men's Surgical by any chance? I've just phoned through to the ward and they say someone should be down here.'

'Yes, Staff, I brought Mr Davison to theatre, he's due in next.'

'Well don't disappear just yet. We have one of your gentlemen still in the recovery room.' She consulted her notes. 'A Mr West, removal of a tumour, which was non-malignant by the way. The op went fine, everything according to plan, but he's taking a little longer to come round than usual so we've been keeping an eye on him. Can you hang on and escort him back to the ward. It shouldn't be long. He's just beginning to stir and take notice.'

'Yes, Staff.'

'Fine, just go into the recovery room over there. The porters will be in in a few minutes. If you'd like to stay with him I'll just go and check on the emergency which is on its way in.' She tutted. 'This is going to upset things and Mr Drummond isn't going to like it. He hates having his lists messed around with, as he puts it. Still, it can't be helped. We're already at full stretch.' She hurried away, a small mauve-clad figure, and it was half an hour later that Emma finally managed to get back to the ward, feeling the knot of tension tightening in her stomach the moment she reached the doors.

To her relief, however, there was no sign of Garrard Blair, but Sue, whizzing past her bearing a bedpan, managed to mutter, 'I think Mr Blair was hoping to see you. I did explain that you'd taken a patient to theatre.'

'I saw him on the way up.'

'Well he didn't seem particularly pleased when you didn't get back before the end of his round. I somehow got the feeling it was fairly urgent.'

Emma purposefully lowered her head over the dressings trolley. 'Yes, well I dare say if it is he'll be in touch later.'

Sue looked at her, slightly incredulous and obviously wanting to talk, but Emma didn't feel inclined to enlighten her. As for Garrard Blair, if he thought she was going to keep the farce going to the extent of appearing in public as a loving couple, well he had another think coming. Her fingers tightened on the pair of suture scissors she was holding and, with a sigh of exasperation, Sue hurried away.

For the rest of the day Emma managed to keep busy, even during those times which would normally have allowed a slight lull in the pace. She was in no hurry to get away despite the fact that it had been her long day and she didn't finish until eight. Collecting her cape she made her way downstairs, promising herself a long soak in a hot bath, and was just on her way towards the exit doors when she saw a tall figure in the distance. Her steps faltered as, even from the far end of the corridor, without being able to see his features clearly, she knew it was Garrard Blair. She caught herself actually on the point of flight and forced herself to stand still. He was engrossed in conversation with one of his colleagues and if she marched straight ahead, pretending to be lost in her own thoughts there was just a possibility that she might manage to slip past without being seen.

Fixing her eyes firmly ahead she walked down the corridor, hoping that the misery she felt wasn't showing on her face. It was a vain hope. Just as she drew level the dark head rose. She saw him hesitate and raise his hand in her direction, urging her to wait. Without thinking she quickened her steps and almost ran. His voice called after her. In the same instant she saw Mike Richards come round the corner and hurried towards him.

'Emma wait, I have to talk to you.'

Relentlessly she ignored the call.

'Mike, wait, I'm going your way.'

He paused, looked at her stricken face, then her arm was linked in his and fixing a smile on her face she turned and called, 'Sorry, I have to rush. Will it wait 'til later?'

'No, Emma, it won't.' The man at his side was still talking. It was a cowardly thing to do but she took the only way out—waved and took Mike's arm, virtually propelling him down the steps, and only when they had reached the safety of the car-park did she slow down, breathing hard with the almost hysterical pounding of her heart.

She had been unforgivably rude but if she was honest with herself, even the thought of his anger was preferable to the misery of having to endure his presence. She raced on, gulping in the fresh air and it was Mike's hand which eventually stopped her in her tracks.

'Hey, how about slowing down a bit.'

She blinked, realising that she had almost been running. 'Sorry.'

'For heaven's sake, where's the fire?' His smile faded. 'I suppose you realise what you just did?'

She leaned weakly against a wall, telling herself firmly that she wasn't going to faint. 'Yes, I suppose I do. Oh Mike, bless you for coming along when you did.'

He studied her quizzically. 'Something tells me I've just walked into a situation I shall wish I'd avoided.' He frowned. 'I shall probably be a marked man from now on'. He saw her startled gaze fly up to his and laughed. 'I'm joking. All the same, the Great White Chief didn't look exactly pleased. Did you have to make it look quite as if we had a secret assignation?'

She stared at him miserably, the full implication of what she had done only now fully dawning. 'Oh Mike, I really am sorry.' Her nose prickled as tears welled up. 'I shouldn't have involved you.'

'Well now that I am involved how about telling me what it's all about for a start.'

She gulped hard. 'I don't think I can. I'm just being silly.'

'I'd say it's probably just a case of engagement nerves. It does happen you know, or so I'm told.'

The kindness in his voice was just about too much and the irony of what he had said drew a choking sob from her before she buried her face against his jacket. Vaguely she heard a car drive past, far too quickly, pausing at the hospital gates before screeching off down the road, and was glad she had been spared the humiliation of anyone else witnessing the undoubted spectacle she was making of herself.

'Here, come on.' Mike proffered his hanky and nodded in the direction of the disappearing car. 'I think the big bad wolf has just gone.'

'Wh . . . what do you mean?'

'I rather think that was our Mr Blair, apparently in a tearing hurry.'

'Oh no.' Horror widened her eyes.

'Don't worry, I don't think he saw you.'

'I wouldn't count on it,' she muttered crossly, sniffing hard. 'Oh dear, I only seem to make things worse.'

Look, how about some coffee and food? I haven't eaten all day. I don't suppose you have either.

It might make you feel better and if it will help you can tell me all about it.' His mouth smiled but she could see the strangely wistful look in his eyes and it made her hesitate. The only thing she really wanted was to crawl into bed and have a good cry.

'It's only coffee I'm offering,' Mike said, gently, 'and food. Nothing else. I'm not the kind who treads on someone else's territory, however much I might be tempted.'

It was some seconds before the meaning of his words sank in and she looked up, blushing, and dashed the tears from her eyes. Why not, she thought with sudden recklessness, after all, Garrard Blair's ring didn't give him any claims on her. He himself had made that perfectly clear. Besides which, she had no intention of starving herself to death for him. Her chin rose.

'As a matter of fact I'd love to. But I'd have to change first. We aren't allowed out in our uniforms.'

'That's okay. I have to change too. Why don't we make it in half an hour. We can go somewhere quiet and talk if you want to, or not, whichever you like.'

Some sudden impulse made her stand on tiptoe and kiss him on the cheek, then before he could say anything she turned and fled across to the Nurses' Home, thinking how much less complicated life would be if only she could have fallen in love with someone like Mike.

CHAPTER FIFTEEN

MIKE was waiting for her when she came down the steps half an hour later. She had changed into a soft, blue woollen dress, swallowed a couple of aspirin which had still not entirely managed to control a dull headache, and brushed her hair. A glance in the mirror had shown a white face with eyes smudged by shadows, and she gave a sigh of quiet relief that the restaurant lighting was subdued. Even so she eased the candle away fractionally as its brilliance irritated the soreness of her eyes.

The waiter handed Mike a menu and left them to make their choice. 'I like it here. It's busy but never noisy and the food's good.' Mike glanced at her. 'Do you think you could manage something?'

Emma felt her stomach churn but managed to smile grimly. It was ridiculous to let Garrard Blair affect her like this. 'Mm, ravenous,' she lied, enthusiastically.

'Any particular preferences?'

'After hospital food? I'd be spoilt for choice.'

He grinned. 'I know what you mean. Shall we settle for steaks?'

She was only too happy to leave the choice to him and sat back as he gave their order to the waiter. When their food arrived, however, she stared with dismay at the array of meat and beautifully fresh vegetables which, at any other time, would have made her mouth water. But suddenly her normally healthy appetite had deserted her and she picked her way through it, making appreciative noises and sipping at her wine until Mike gave her a sidelong look and putting down his fork said gently, 'You're not really hungry are you?'

She stared at the plate, appalled to see how little impression she had made on it, and protested violently, 'Oh but I am. It's delicious. I love steak.'

'So why do I get the distinct impression that you wouldn't know it from chaff just at this moment?' Mike shook his head. 'A snail would have made more progress round that plate, Emma. Why didn't you just say you're not hungry, I wouldn't have minded.'

She put her knife and fork down, swallowing hard on the lump in her throat, and stared desolately at the sweet trolley laden with delicacies for which at any other time she would have dieted for a month. 'I'm sorry. I just can't seem to manage it.'

Mike's hand came to rest over hers. 'You seem to have developed a habit of always apologising and there's no need. Would you like coffee and a talk, or would you rather we just pretended everything was fine?'

She kept her head lowered as the waiter whisked her plate away and coffee appeared.

'I'm a good listener you know. Of course I don't know much about marriage counselling but I have it on fairly good authority that pre-wedding nerves are a prerequisite for all brides. You'd be surprised how many times I've given my shoulder to be wept on. Here, it's this one, you'll notice it's a shade lower than the other.'

She giggled and sniffed and then, to her horror, felt a tear roll down her cheek. 'Idiot.'

He didn't smile. 'I'd like to help, Emma. I'm sure it can't be that bad. Or can it?' He waited and when she didn't answer said, 'I thought being engaged was supposed to be the best time of a girl's life, or have I been getting it wrong all these years?'

Even the word 'engaged' was like a raw wound into which, unknowingly, he had flung salt.

Tears coursed slowly down her cheeks. 'I'm sure you're right. The trouble is, I'm not . . . engaged, that is.'

She knew he was staring at her. 'I don't think I understand. I mean, it's all over the hospital.'

'Yes of course it is,' she snapped, peeling another tissue from her bag and abandoning a sodden one. 'Because that's what he wanted. Only it isn't real.'

He was frowning, leaning across the table to hold her shaking hand. 'Look, I may be a bit dim, but none of this makes sense.'

'Well I know that.'

'So suppose you try explaining. Are you engaged or not? Did he give you a ring and ask you to marry him, it's really that simple.'

She detached her hand from his and blew her nose hard. 'No it isn't. Yes, he gave me a ring,' she tugged the chain from round her neck and held the diamond for him to see, 'and we are engaged but we're not getting married.'

Mike gave a sigh of exasperation. 'This isn't getting any clearer, Emma.'

'No,' she sighed heavily, 'I don't suppose it is, but don't you see it's just pretend. Something we

. . . he thought up to avoid the gossip.'

'I hadn't realised there was any.'

She stared at him, her eyes widening. 'But you must have. Everyone else did. It started after he rescued me from Phil Carrington and I was upset, so he drove me to his flat and because it was late and I was still very shocked, I stayed the night. On the couch,' she added defiantly.

'I believe you.'

'Yes, well you would,' she said it with a surge of tenderness for him. 'But no one else did. You know what the hospital grapevine is like.'

'And you mean he came up with this idea of an engagement just to put an end to the gossip.' Mike studied her pale face shrewdly. 'Doesn't it strike you as a bit drastic?'

'Well I suppose it is, but he was right in a way. At least it made things seem . . . well it didn't seem quite so sordid somehow, and anyway, he's already in love with someone else and I should think the last thing he wants is a lot of stories being spread around.'

'And you think the fact that he appears to be engaged to you would make it right?' Mike sat back. 'I suppose you're absolutely sure you've understood his motives?'

'Oh yes.' Emma blinked. Of course she had. What other possible motive could there be?

'Well all I can say is Blair must be mad. Either that or he's a very cold fish.'

'No, oh no, he isn't. He's a marvellous doctor. I've seen him with his patients. He cares, deeply.' She reddened as the words came out in a rush and Mike frowned pityingly.

'Poor Emma, you've really got it badly, haven't you?'

'I don't know what you mean.' She was glad of the subtle lighting which at least hid her partially from the other diners.

'Oh come on, I think you do. You're in love with the man, Emma. It's as plain as the nose on your face, and a very pretty nose it is too.' He had her hand again and Emma looked up into his eyes as he put her fingers to his lips, kissing them gently. 'I'm afraid I don't know what to say, except that the man has to be crazy. I know if I were in his place . . .'

She was never to know what would happen if he were because as she looked quickly away in hot embarrassment, her gaze seemed to lock with that of the man across the room, and for one heart-freezing moment the room seemed to revolve around her. Her mouth went dry with shock as she saw Garrard Blair staring with a glacial expression in their direction and knew without any words that he had witnessed every moment of what had passed between herself and Mike.

Her mind raced, seeing it all like a camera in slow sequence, imagining what interpretation he must have put on it. Her lips moved as she wanted to tell him it wasn't true, but no sound came and she heard Mike say, 'Emma, what is it?'

She shook her head, unable to answer, and half rose to her feet just as the woman seated across the table from Garrard turned to look in her direction, a smile on her beautiful face.

Emma felt the anger rise in her like a tide as she reached for her bag and stumbled to her feet. So the pretence was only important when he found it convenient. Right now she wasn't sure whether the anger she saw on his face was because she had caught him out or because she had failed to keep to her own part of the bargain, but she had no intention of waiting to find out.

'Please, Mike, can we go?' He was beside her as she reached out blindly for his arm. She saw that Garrard had risen to his feet and that his icy gaze watched their departure. She only prayed he wouldn't try to prevent it as she made for the door, afraid to look back.

It wasn't until she was seated safely in Mike's car that her heart beat began to get slowly back to normal, and only then did she realise that she wasn't going to be able to avoid Garrard Blair for ever.

CHAPTER SIXTEEN

SISTER was in a bad mood next morning. A mood which seemed to affect everyone, and consequently everyone was kept on their toes and everything, ironically, seemed to go wrong.

One patient due for an op had to be cancelled at the last minute when it was discovered he had a throat infection which he had been surreptitiously trying to conceal by sucking lozenges, until his temperature soared and he earned a stern lecture for his pains and was promptly ordered home. Then theatre rang through at mid-morning, putting back the entire list because of emergency admissions following a nasty pile-up on the busy main road just a few blocks from the hospital.

'We're taking them because we have the facilities,' Theatre Sister explained. 'I know we're practically full to overflowing but it's better they come here than have to be taken fifteen miles to St James's. One of them will be coming to you. It looks like a fracture of the spine from the information we've had so far but we'll know more when we've had him in theatre and taken a proper look. Two others are for Women's Surgical and one other looks as if he isn't going to make it anywhere. He's in a pretty bad way but perhaps you'd better be ready, just in case.'

Emma stood silently as Sister Meredith listened and finally said, 'Don't worry, we'll cope, some-

how. As it happens we have one patient who is
being sent home anyway because of an infection
and he'll be re-admitted at a later date. Just let me
know when you're sending him up will you, Sister?'
She put the phone down, rubbed at her eyes for
a moment then studied Emma. 'Nurse Benedict,
ah yes,' her expression darkened as she frowned
at the girl before her. 'I trust I am not to take the
request which appeared on my desk this morning
seriously?'

Emma quailed before the expression of rigid
disapproval and had to force herself not to beg her
pardon, admit it was all a mistake and run.

She clasped her hands behind her to prevent
them shaking. It had taken hours of tossing and
turning and thinking through the night to bring her
to the point of doing what she had done and she
couldn't be thwarted now. 'It . . . it's a request for a
transfer, Sister, to another ward . . . Women's
Orthopaedic if possible.' She said it at random,
anywhere where she wouldn't have to come into
daily contact with Garrard Blair.

'I am perfectly well aware what it is, Nurse. What
I find hard to understand is how you can expect me
to treat it seriously. Have you any idea of what
would happen if I were to arrange for members of
staff to be moved just when it suited them, and for
no apparent reason other than that they feel like a
change?'

Emma squirmed. 'But I do have reasons, Sister.
Very good reasons.' Please just don't ask me to
explain them, she prayed silently.

'I'm sure you think you do, Nurse, however, I
can assure you that nothing can be considered more

important than the smooth running of this ward and I have absolutely no intention of upsetting either that routine or the routine of this hospital in order to accommodate you. Apart from the fact that nurses do not take it upon themselves to choose where they shall work, to transfer you now would mean that another nurse would have to be brought in to replace you, which would also disrupt another ward not to mention her own training. No, I'm sorry, Nurse, it is out of the question. You will complete your three months on Men's Surgical and then it will be up to someone else to decide where you go next.' Sister Meredith rose to her feet. 'I am extremely disappointed in you, Nurse. Now, please get back to the ward, there are patients still requiring your attention and regardless of your personal preferences, whilst you remain a nurse at this hospital, you will continue to abide by its rules.'

Emma felt herself dismissed with scarcely a look but there was a wealth of contempt in the single gesture of her hand. Making her way miserably back to the ward, Emma plunged herself into a desperate round of bed making which unfortunately did nothing more than leave her feeling exhausted and bad tempered. And then she was made to swab the lockers all over again because Staff Nurse Blake wasn't satisfied with them.

She was in the midst of this and doing it with very bad grace when a solitary male figure walked on to the ward. She felt her knees suddenly go weak and steeled herself for the confrontation which was bound to come, but apart from one single, frozen glance in her direction he ignored her completely and disappeared into Sister's office from which he emerged minutes later looking decidedly crosser than ever to begin his round.

Emma gathered up her cloths and the bowl and fled to the kitchen. Had he taken his girlfriend home last night, she wondered as she rinsed the suds vigorously away, wishing she could wash Garrard Blair just as easily out of her life. Had they fallen into each other's arms and arranged the date of their wedding?

She closed her eyes, wondering why she tormented herself with such thoughts then opened them with a start as the doors opened and she heard her own gasp of horror as he stood there, a look of cold savagery on his face.

'G—Garrard . . . Mr Blair . . . sir.'

'Don't give me that, Emma.' He saw her flinch. 'I want to talk to you.'

She had instinctively backed away until she stood now, pressed up against the sink. 'I'm very busy.'

'Don't play games with me, Emma, you won't win.' His voice was brittle with anger. 'I've spoken to Sister. You're due for your coffee break anyway and I insist on speaking to you this time, alone, so you may as well accept it.'

It half crossed her mind to protest that she had to finish some other job, or say she had to take a patient to theatre, only to have the words die on her lips as the look in his eye told her that he was perfectly capable of reading her thoughts and wasn't about to brook any arguments.

He held the door open. 'My room, Emma.'

She went ahead of him, purposely avoiding his eyes and just as she was wondering if she could escape, his hand closed on her arm and she found herself almost forced into the room he used as an office. She stood, wishing her legs would stop shaking and that he would move away from the door.

'Well, Emma, this time I've made sure you can't avoid me as you have been doing these past few days, for reasons best known to yourself. I'd like to be enlightened, if you don't mind.'

She felt her cheeks burn. 'I don't know what you mean.'

His brow rose and he looked at her, coolly. 'It won't work, Emma. Each time you've seen me and I've tried to talk to you you've scuttled away like a nervous rabbit and then last night . . . I take it you do have an explanation for last night?'

Her chin rose. 'I don't see that any explanation is necessary,' she began, and realised at once as the muscle in his jaw twitched, that she had made a grave error.

'Don't you indeed?' He had moved from the door and now came towards her. 'Oh but I think you do, Emma, and I want to know what's going on. In fact, you don't leave here until I've found out.'

She gasped. 'But you can't keep me here. I have to get back to the ward and anyway, you have no right.'

'It's up to you. I can keep you here perfectly well and you know it, and I will, unless you give me some explanation—and it had better be good.'

Anger began to mingle with resentment. 'I fail to see that you have any right to dictate my actions, or who I see when I'm off-duty. Mike Richards is a friend and I shall go out with whoever I please.'

'On the contrary, Emma,' he was now so close

that she shivered. 'What you do is very much my affair and I have every right to object to your going out with another man.' His hands gripped her arms. 'In case it has slipped your memory, you are engaged to me.'

Her head jerked up furiously. 'And in case you have forgotten, our "engagement" as you choose to call it, is nothing more than a farce, an . . . arrangement of convenience. Well frankly I don't find it at all convenient and from what I also saw last night, I wouldn't have thought you did either. Or am I supposed to turn a blind eye to your own little . . .'

'Don't say it, Emma.' His eyes narrowed and for one moment she steeled herself for the fury she saw in them. 'You don't need to concern yourself with who I see, Emma, it has nothing to do with our arrangement.'

'Well I happen to think it has.' She flung the words at him and tugged at the chain round her neck, breaking the clasp with the force of it. 'As far as I'm concerned our little arrangement is over and you can take your ring back.'

She held out her hand and felt an incredible feeling of dread sweep over her as he looked at the diamond, an unreadable expression on his face.

'Oh no, Emma. I'm afraid I'm not going to make it that easy for you.'

He made no move to take the ring and she stared at him. 'What do you mean?'

'I mean that we made a bargain.'

'But you don't even want to be engaged to me and I . . . I hate you.' She thrust the ring at him again. 'I don't want to be engaged to you.'

His face was taut. 'Well that's a pity because I'm afraid I don't find it convenient yet to put an end to it, so for the moment at least you'll just have to put up with it.' Suddenly he reached out and drew her closer, his hands biting into the flesh of her arms. '*I* will decide when it comes to an end, Emma, and that time isn't yet.' Suddenly he swooped and his mouth locked angrily with hers. It was a punishing kiss, brutal, careless of the pain which made her lips part involuntarily in a gasp beneath his. For an instant he seemed to relent as her eyes filled with tears and she swayed against him, longingly, willingly. He released her abruptly. 'You'd better go.'

White-faced she looked at him.

'Just remember, Emma, *I* decide and until I do, you're engaged to me.' He held the door open and she walked out, trembling with anger and shock. It was only as she turned towards the stairs that she realised she still had the ring clasped in her hand, and when she looked it had cut cruelly into her palm. One way or another, she thought, Garrard Blair would leave his mark and no matter what happened, she was the one who was going to get hurt.

She tossed and turned for a long time that night, getting up to make herself a cup of cocoa then going back to bed only to fall into a heavy sleep from which she woke feeling drugged and bad tempered. The only consolation was that at least now she saw the answer, the only sure way, and that was to leave St Clement's altogether, to get right away to some place where she might be able to gather up the pieces and some day make a fresh start.

It was her morning off but instead of catching up on chores or taking advantage of it to have a lie in, she got up, bathed and put on her uniform and an hour before she had to go on duty was tapping on the door of the Director of Nursing Services.

Right up to the last minute she had wondered whether she would have the courage to go through with it. St Clement's had become part of her life, she loved it and leaving was going to mean saying goodbye to a lot of people who had become friends, and yet what future was there for her here. She sighed. Why couldn't she have fallen in love with some ordinary, uncomplicated man, like Mike for instance?

She tapped at the door before she could change her mind and Miss Baxter's voice beckoned her in.

She entered and the woman behind the desk looked up smiling. 'Nurse . . . Benedict, isn't it? Yes, Nurse, what can I do for you?'

Emma stood uncertainly and Miss Baxter's neatly defined brows rose fractionally. In her mid-fifties she was still a very attractive woman and could easily have passed for forty.

'Is there some problem I can help you with?' She prompted gently, and Emma bit her lip, realising that all the words she had so carefully rehearsed had gone completely out of her head.

'I . . . I . . . yes. That is . . .'

'Perhaps you'd better sit down and tell me about it.'

Emma obeyed, sitting in the large chair and staring at her hands. 'I came to give in my notice. I realise the normal requirement is for one month but if there is any way it can be arranged without causing too much inconvenience, I would very much like to leave as soon as possible.'

Miss Baxter's frown of concern was genuine. 'I'm very sorry to hear this, Nurse.' She rose to her feet and crossed to a large cabinet taking a file from it. 'Is there something you would care to talk about? Perhaps something I can help you with?'

Emma thought about it then shook her head. 'No, I don't think so.'

'Well would you care to give me some reason for this rather sudden decision? I take it it is sudden.'

'Oh yes, at least . . . yes it is.'

'I see.' Miss Baxter sat again and opened the file. 'Is it that you're not happy with us?' She consulted the papers in front of her. 'Your work has always been up to standard, apart from one or two teething troubles, but those are to be expected.' She looked up. 'Or have you decided that nursing is simply not what you wish to do after all?'

Emma found herself almost wishing that were true but she shook her head. 'No, it isn't that. I love it at Clems—I mean St Clement's—it's just that I have . . . personal reasons for wishing to leave as soon as possible.'

Miss Baxter's faintly pastelled lips smiled. 'Are you sure they are really so urgent that you have to give in your notice? We shall be very sorry to lose you.' She waited. 'Won't you at least consider staying with us until you get married?' She was unprepared for the look of acute misery which flooded the girl's face and she saw the sudden tensing of her hands.

'No, I really can't change my plans. I'm sorry.'

'My dear, I have no wish to pry, but I do understand that there are times when one's friends and colleagues can tease, and with the best will in the world it all becomes too much. I think I understand what it must be like for you. Mr Blair is a much respected figure here and it is only natural that people will take an interest in things which concern him but we are all very happy for you both. If it is simply a matter of transferring you temporarily to another ward I'm sure if Sister had understood . . .' she broke off. 'Yes, Sister did talk to me about your request, naturally, but under the circumstances I'm sure we could arrange something.'

Emma felt her heart give a slight leap. 'I would like to be transferred but I'm afraid it changes nothing. I still intend giving in my notice.'

The older woman nodded, her eyes briefly clouding with disappointment. 'Well if you've made your decision I can only say that I am very sorry. Of course I must accept it if you insist.' She reached for a list pinned to the notice board behind her. 'I can move you to Women's Surgical. It will mean working nights I'm afraid but they are short-handed anyway. If that will help?'

'Oh yes.'

'Fine. I suggest you go across there tomorrow then. I'll speak to Sister Meredith and find her a replacement.'

Emma rose to her feet. The interview was at an end and she felt as if she carried a lead yoke on her shoulders, but at least she had done it. Now all that mattered was to survive the next month.

CHAPTER SEVENTEEN

THERE was something very strange about going on duty when it was dark and everyone else was just going home to have an evening meal and look forward to falling into bed. It was something Emma wondered if she would ever get used to as she wandered along to the cafeteria at midnight to have 'breakfast'. Not that she was likely to find out now, so it didn't matter anyway, but after her first week of night duty she was still finding it difficult to adjust. The only good thing about it was that she hadn't seen Garrard.

Depression enveloped her like a huge cloud as she helped herself to scrambled eggs and went to sit at a table by herself. The cafeteria was seldom crowded at night. Staff came and went whenever the wards were quiet. In a perverse sort of way she almost missed the bustle that went with day duties. It had meant she had less time to think, to wonder if he had even noticed that she wasn't there. Probably not, she decided and ate her way through her breakfast without really noticing it.

Piling her empty crockery on to a tray she resigned herself to going back to the ward. The question of what she would do after she left St Clement's still had to be decided and was still being pushed to the back of her mind. She had written several applications but so far nothing had resulted from them and she wasn't even sure that she wanted a solution, not just yet. What she needed was time to think, to forget, just to get away.

She roused herself and went back to the ward just as Staff Nurse Barker came towards her. 'Ah, Nurse, thank heavens you're back. It looks as if we're in for a busy night after all. Just when I'd thought we might get a quiet one for a change. I might have known it was too good to last.'

Emma was immediately alert, pushing away all thoughts except those which involved her work. 'What's happened, Staff?'

'We have an emergency on its way in. I don't have the full details yet but Mr Blair rang through personally and asked for a side-ward to be got ready.'

Emma felt her heart lurch as she followed Staff's bustling figure along the ward. 'Mr Blair, Staff?'

'That's right.' Staff lowered her voice because of the sleeping patients. 'I gather the patient is Sir James Halston's daughter and he happened to be with her. Anyway the ambulance is on its way in and he's following it, hence the flap, so let's scoot to it, Nurse. We're lucky the side-ward is empty. Make sure the bed is warm.'

Their soft-soled shoes made scarcely any sound as they walked between the rows of beds towards the dim light of the small office. 'Nurse Granger is getting the examination kit ready. Dr MacGregor is duty House Surgeon. I imagine he'll be up to see the patient fairly quickly.'

Emma performed her tasks automatically, like some sort of robot, she thought. It was all like something out of a nightmare and however much she tried to wake herself out of it she couldn't. The bitter irony of the situation kept on pursuing her.

It seemed like hours before the ambulance came through the gates, blue light flashing, though in fact it was only minutes. From the window she saw it draw to a halt, the car behind following, a tall figure leaping out as the ambulance doors were swung open. In spite of everything her heart went out to him as she imagined what he must be going through, having to see the woman he loved in pain. Then she drew herself up and moved quickly away from the window. She was a nurse and a patient was being brought in and must be treated as any other patient, except that this one wouldn't be the same.

With a kind of ruthless determination she hadn't known she was capable of she turned her efforts to her work, and there was time for nothing else as the trolley was wheeled in and Emma drew back the covers on the bed and stood back, waiting as people moved, hurriedly but calmly. She caught only a brief glimpse of the girl as she was lifted into the bed. Her face was ashen and her skin clammy as she groaned with pain. Emma moved to hand the chart to Staff and suddenly caught the look of anguish on the face of the man who had moved silently to the bedside. It shocked her and she didn't think he had even noticed her despite the fact that his glance passed over her once, briefly, before he was back with the girl, his voice terse as he took charge.

'Who's on duty?'

'Dr MacGregor, sir. I've already telephoned him and he's on his way up.' Staff supplied the information briskly.

The girl moaned, biting her lip, and Emma watched as her hand clung to Garrard's.

'For God's sake, where is he?'

She flinched at the note of anger in his voice and turned away as the door opened and the House Surgeon came in, but not before she had seen the beautiful diamond and emerald ring on the girl's finger.

'I'm pretty sure it's the appendix,' she heard Garrard say. 'I think it's close to perforating. Is there a theatre free?'

The House Surgeon bent to make his own examination and nodded confirmation. 'I checked before I came along. Theatre Two is ready. I agree, this is going to need pretty prompt attention. The tenderness is very marked.' He looked at Staff. 'Get the patient ready will you, give the pre-med as soon as you can and we'll get her along to theatre straight away.' He looked up. 'I take it Sir James isn't here?'

Emma saw Garrard brush a hand through his hair. 'No, I advised him to stay by the phone. I'll call him as soon as there's any news.'

'Mm, well that won't be for some time yet.'

They moved away and Emma moved automatically to straighten the covers and take the patient's pulse. For a moment her gaze rose and locked with Garrard's as he turned. Of course she didn't need to be told that the look of acute misery she saw was for the girl she was tending, but there was no time to think about it then and she was reaching for the thermometer as he turned and strode away. Out of my life for ever, she thought.

She was relieved when one of the other nurses escorted Jane Halston up to theatre. There was no sign of Garrard, he had probably disappeared to wait for news, she thought, wishing again, fleetingly, that there was something she could do to relieve his anxiety.

The next hour was spent in reassuring patients who had been wakened by the comings and goings, handing out bedpans and generally restoring peace and quiet, which wasn't easy when several of the ladies complained grumpily that they wouldn't be able to close their eyes again for the rest of the night. It was some consolation to find them snoring their heads off half an hour later when Emma walked by their beds.

It was four o'clock before the trolley was wheeled back on to the ward. Jane Halston was still pale but sleeping off the effects of the anaesthetic and at least the cause of the pain would have been removed.

Emma was just drawing the curtains around the bed when Garrard walked into the side-room, and she managed to slip quickly away from the direct light cast by the small overhead lamp as he drew up a chair and sat by the bed, taking the girl's hand gently in his. She left the room, closing the door quietly behind her and had to bite her lip to hold back the tears as she glanced through the glass window and saw them together.

Staff Nurse Barker's voice jerked her back to reality. 'You can take your coffee break now, Nurse, while we're quiet. Nurse Granger has just come back.'

'Yes, Staff.'

She cast one last look into the dimly-lit room just as Garrard looked up. He frowned and for a moment she thought he was actually going to get to his feet, then she turned and sped off the ward and down the stairs to the coffee lounge, fighting an immense wave of depression which suddenly engulfed her. It was probably nothing more than sheer, physical tiredness she told herself. It always seemed to hit during the early hours of the morning in the lull just before daylight when the ward reached its busiest peak again and before the Day Staff came on.

The coffee lounge was quite busy now. Most nurses seemed to feel the need to revive themselves with copious drinks and she resigned herself to being drawn into the chatter even though her mind was still back on Women's Surgical. She sank into one of the large leather chairs, drank the scalding hot coffee and stared into space, letting the noise gather around her. There was no longer any need to keep up the pretence, she thought. She knew it from the look in his eyes and he must know it too. Well there was only one thing left to do. Putting down her cup she unfastened the chain from round her neck and slipped the ring into her pocket. At least she could save them both the embarrassment of having him ask for its return. He had said he would decide when the time had come, well it had to be now. He had got what he wanted, she could only hope he would be happy. In sudden misery she reached for her cup again, before she could ask herself when there would ever be any happiness in her own life again. Perhaps with a bit of luck she might be able to persuade Miss Baxter to let her go before the month was up after all, if she pleaded compassionate grounds. Her mouth twisted wryly.

Passionate grounds would be more like it, except that the passion had been too one-sided.

She heard her name being spoken and responded dully to the talk around her. Finishing her coffee she made the excuse that she had to get back to the ward and turned her steps along the corridor towards the stairs. It wouldn't be for much longer, she thought, and knew that she was going to miss it more than she had ever missed anything in her life.

Someone came towards her but it wasn't until Sally stopped in front of her, smiling as she spoke, that she came to with a start.

'I heard you were on nights and I'd been hoping I'd see you,' Sally bubbled over with vivacious enthusiasm. 'I heard your marvellous news too. Gosh you're a dark horse, Benedict. Why on earth didn't you say something? I've been going out of my mind wanting to hear all the details. Not that I blame you mind. I'd want to keep a dish like that quiet. So when's the happy day to be? You are going to send me an invite I hope? I'll even be bridesmaid.'

Emma stared at her, wondering how she could put her present misery into words without bursting into tears. She tried to raise a smile and failed, and anyway, what was the use? Her throat ached with the need to cry but that was something she would have to save until later, much later.

She stood, vaguely mouthing words that wouldn't come, seeing Sally's smiling face in front of her, and then knew that someone came to stand behind her. For a moment it didn't register until a hand came to rest lightly on her shoulder and she felt herself freeze.

Her anguished gaze flew up to meet Garrard's and she saw the brief question in his eyes, noted the grey lines of exhaustion before he spoke. How could he sound so calm, she wondered. But then, that was all part of the game they had agreed on. Play a part, keep the charade going just long enough and then end it, just like that, without any emotion, except that she was being torn apart inside.

He smiled at Sally. 'As a matter of fact we haven't named the day but I'm not a believer in long engagements, so you can draw your own conclusions from that.'

Emma felt a kind of dull pain shoot through her, followed by anger as his hand came firmly under her arm.

'Shall we go, Emma? There's something I have to talk to you about.'

Incapable of saying a word she felt herself propelled forward and out through the doors. He didn't believe in long engagements. No, well he wouldn't. He had obviously intended that theirs should be as brief as possible!

It was the cold air hitting her that jerked her back to life and the realisation that he was looking at her carefully. She held back, trying to free herself from his grasp. 'Where are you taking me? I'm supposed to be on duty.'

'That's all right, I fixed things with Sister. I want to talk to you.'

She braced herself, shaking him off as she faced him, battling with all the pent-up emotions she had struggled for so long to contain.

'There's really nothing to say. I have your ring

here.' She held out her hand and it lay in the palm, glittering like ice and equally as cold, she thought. 'I was going to bring it along to you anyway.'

He stared at it and at her but made no move to take it. Instead he put his hands on her shoulders, taking her relentlessly along with him. 'I don't want it, Emma. What I want is to talk to you, to know why you ran away from me. Why you gave in your notice. Did you really think you could escape that easily?'

He was looking at her, forcing her to face him, and she couldn't speak. He shook her gently. 'Emma, what's wrong?'

'Wrong?' She laughed but it sounded more like a sob. How could he keep up the pretence? She tried to break free. 'Why should anything be wrong?'

He almost shook her. 'I don't understand, Emma.'

'Oh please, don't let's go on pretending. It's really quite simple. I'm ending our engagement.'

His expression was rigid. 'I wasn't aware that we had been pretending, Emma.'

Her hands clenched as she faced him. 'How can you say that? Hasn't it been a pretence right from the start? You said yourself we would call it off . . .'

'Because I was under the impression that that was what you wanted.' His voice was very quiet and there was something very disturbing about the dark, enigmatic gaze as he looked at her. '*Is* that what you want, Emma?'

Words died in the tightness of her throat and she turned away. No, of course it wasn't. Couldn't he see that? His hand came down lightly on her shoulder and she swallowed hard, biting back the tears. What more did he want? He had the ring. He was free. Why didn't he just go?

'I asked you a question, Emma. I think you at least owe me an answer, don't you?' He turned her to face him, gently tilting her head back so that she had to look at him.

'It's perfectly simple.' She closed her eyes and felt a tear ooze out and trickle down her cheek. 'I don't see any point in keeping up the pretence any longer when . . . when you have every intention of marrying someone else. Well now you're perfectly free. I'm trying to save you any embarrassment. Can't you at least do the same for me? I thought two adult people could at least be civilised.'

His eyes narrowed as he looked at her. 'You realise of course that I haven't the slightest idea what you're talking about.'

'Oh for pity's sake,' she was shouting and she knew it. 'What more do you want from me? It's perfectly obvious to everyone that you're in love with Sir James's daughter and are going to marry her.'

'Sir J . . . Is this some kind of joke, Emma, because if so I don't find it funny.' His expression barely changed yet his voice was so cold that she shivered.

'I don't see any reason to joke.'

'Then I'm glad because neither do I. Quite the contrary. I dislike the thought that I'm the subject of gossip and in particular of gossip which is incorrect.'

She gasped. 'But it isn't. Everyone knows you were engaged to her and that she broke off the engagement. I also saw you with her when she was brought in and I'm not blind. I could see for myself that you were worried sick.' She sniffed hard. 'I just think it was very cruel of you to use me to make her jealous and anyway, if you had any sense at all you might have known that a person like that couldn't possibly be jealous of someone like me. It's qu . . . quite ridiculous.'

For a long time he didn't answer then she heard him make a strange, explosive sound in his throat before something quite incredible happened.

'My dear Emma, yes you're right, I was worried sick. I've known Jane and her father for many years. They are very close friends.' He paused then went on. 'It is also true that I was engaged to her, but what you don't seem to understand is that our engagement was ended by mutual consent, because we both agreed that, deep as our feelings were, they were not love, and it may interest you to know that Jane is now engaged to a young, very dashing army captain who has every intention of marrying her and whisking her away overseas as soon as possible. It so happens that he is abroad right now, which is why he isn't here in person. But that is the only reason why I am here now.'

She couldn't speak for all the dozens of emotions which seemed to be flooding through her at the same time. Then, without knowing how it happened she was in his arms and he was kissing her and laughing as he wiped away her tears.

'Emma, my darling, don't cry. It makes your face all pink and blotchy and I shall have to keep on kissing you until you stop.'

She sniffed hard again and tried to be angry but

there was something about being in his arms which seemed to make all her resolutions vanish.

'Don't laugh at me,' she snapped crossly.

'I'm not laughing. I'm being very serious.'

She moved her head from his chest just far enough to glance at him suspiciously. 'I don't see anything in the least funny.'

'No, and neither do I, except that I can't imagine how you came to believe such a story.'

Her hands pressed against his chest. 'I'm not sure either, except that I can't think of any other reason why you should want to be engaged to me.'

"You can't?' He held her from him and she saw that he was smiling. 'My dearest girl, the first time I saw you and you nearly broke my fingers in that swing door I decided that it would be far better to have you where I could see you.'

She made a strangled sound of protest which he silenced with a kiss.

'I also decided that I loved you very much.'

She sighed heavily. 'I don't know what to say. I don't think I'm capable of making decisions.'

'Well in that case you must let me make them for you. We'll get married as soon as possible.'

'Oh yes.' She leaned against him dreamily. 'And I suppose this means you'll have to meet my family.'

'I suppose it does.'

'You'll love them and they'll love you. You'll meet my sister.'

He twisted his head to stare at her. 'Sister? Don't tell me there are more at home like you?'

'Oh yes,' she stared at him, wide-eyed. 'But you'll like Pippa. She's the scatty one of the family.'

He made an odd choking sound in his throat, then he kissed her again and she forgot about everything except the fact that she loved him and she thought Sir James' daughter had every reason to be jealous.